Lulu blinked back the tears as she turned to leave. Suddenly, she caught the scent of Old Spice. Sheriff Perkins was standing right behind her. "Young lady," he said, "you are under arrest."

"What? Me?" Lulu gulped.

"Yes, you, Lulu," replied the sheriff gravely.

"What's going on?" Sally called out nervously, hearing them.

"Everything's fine. It's Sheriff Perkins," he answered. "I found your stalker, Sally." He took Lulu's hand. "Come on. I'm taking you down to the station."

I can't believe this is happening! Lulu told herself, trying not to burst into tears. "Celeste!" she whispered, "I need you."

Lulu's
Mixed-Up Movie

ANGEL

CORNERS

Lulu's Mixed-Up Movie

BY FRAN MANUSHKIN

PUFFIN BOOKS

PUFFIN BOOKS
Published by the Penguin Group
Penguin Books USA Inc., 375 Hudson Street, New York, New York 10014, U.S.A.
Penguin Books Ltd, 27 Wrights Lane, London W8 5TZ, England
Penguin Books Australia Ltd, Ringwood, Victoria, Australia
Penguin Books Canada Ltd, 10 Alcorn Avenue, Toronto, Ontario, Canada M4V 3B2
Penguin Books (N.Z.) Ltd, 182–190 Wairau Road, Auckland 10, New Zealand

Penguin Books Ltd, Registered Offices: Harmondsworth, Middlesex, England

First published in the United States of America by Puffin Books,
a division of Penguin Books USA Inc., 1995
Published by arrangement with Chardiet Unlimited, Inc.

1 3 5 7 9 10 8 6 4 2

LIBRARY OF CONGRESS CATALOGING-IN-PUBLICATION DATA
Manushkin, Fran.
Lulu's mixed-up movie / Fran Manushkin.
p.   cm.—(Angel Corners; #3)
Summary: A guardian angel-in-training enters the scene when Lulu
Bliss, discovering her widowed father's interest in another woman,
sets out to capture her competitor's worst side on film.
ISBN 0-14-037200-8
[1. Guardian angels—Fiction.   2. Angels—Fiction.   3. Fathers and
daughters—Fiction.]   I. Title.   II. Series.   III. Series:
Manushkin, Fran. Angel Corners; #3.
PZ7.M3195Lu   1995   [Fic]—dc20   94-49734   CIP   AC

Printed in the United States of America

For Ann-Jeanette Campbell, an angel of an editor!

CONTENTS

Lulu's
Mixed-Up Movie

1

Lulu Bliss, Class Whiz

"A+! A+!" Lulu Bliss chanted. She grabbed Val McCall's hand as they left class together. "This is the first A+ I ever got in my life."

"And you deserved it." Val smiled. "You worked on your Angel Falls video for months."

"It was fun." Lulu's almond-shaped eyes twinkled. "In the summer I got shots of the waterfall with kids swimming nearby. And in October I took pictures of the autumn leaves reflected in it."

Val interrupted. "And remember the day before Christmas when Angel Falls sparkled like an icicle? You leaned way out over the cliff to film it and almost fell off! Aren't you lucky that I was there to grab you?"

"That's what best friends are for." Lulu smiled at Val, who looked as bright and shiny as a new penny with her copper hair and her peach blouse, jeans, and suede lace-up boots.

Val's violet eyes grew dreamy. "Angel Falls looked so romantic in the springtime—like a long lace wedding veil."

Lulu groaned. "Don't you *ever* stop thinking about clothes—or weddings?"

"No." Val smiled good-naturedly. She adored everything to do with clothes and especially weddings.

Lulu was definitely not into weddings, and she liked her clothes comfy and colorful. She was wearing a bright red turtleneck sweater and purple corduroys. She had completed her outfit with one red and one purple sock. Lulu never wore matching socks. They were a total yawn.

"Hey, Val," Lulu said, "did you hear what Ms. Fisher told me today? She said that if I worked this hard in every subject, I'd be a straight-A student."

"That's true," Val agreed. "But you can't make movies for math or spelling class."

"What a shame." Lulu kicked at a stone. "Maybe I could find a way. . . ." She was wild about movies but not so wild about studying. "Hey, look!" she said, happy to change the subject. "Something's happening at the railroad station. There's a crowd.

Let's go see." She grabbed Val's hand and they began running, their matching friendship bracelets jingling.

They soon passed the angel clock, and reached the red-brick railroad station. Mayor Witty's Siberian husky, Hercules, barked wildly as four men in blue overalls leaped down off a truck.

"What's going on?" Lulu asked Mayor Witty.

"You'll know in a minute, young lady." Mayor Witty wiped his plump pink face with a handkerchief and then addressed the crowd: "Fellow citizens of Angel Corners, remember when the town raised money last fall to repair the angel clock?"

"How could we forget?" Lulu whispered in Val's ear. "That was the first project of the Angel Club."

"Well," Mayor Witty rumbled on in his booming voice, "after the angel clock was fixed, tourists began flocking to town to see it. Angel Corners is turning into one of the most popular tourist destinations in New England."

"Yaaay!" Lulu cheered along with the crowd. She was very proud of her little town.

"At last month's town meeting," Mayor Witty continued, "we decided to use the leftover funds to restore the old train station. "These gentlemen here"—the mayor pointed to the four burly men in blue overalls—"are going to sandblast this building until it sparkles. The sandblasting will take about ten days. It's indeed a historical moment for Angel Corners."

Lulu's face lit up. "Val, here's another film I can make. I'll come to the station every day and shoot the workmen."

Mayor Witty overheard her. "Leave those workmen alone, young lady. This is a dangerous construction site. I don't want you to get into trouble."

"I'll be careful," Lulu promised.

Val smiled at her friend. "You get more ideas in a minute than most people do in a year!" That was one of the many reasons Val loved Lulu. Life was never boring around her.

"Hey, look!" Val's face turned bright pink. "There's Zeb Burgess."

"I see." Lulu rolled her eyes. Val had a humongous crush on Zeb, who had hypnotic eyes, curly black hair, and muscles he developed by working out with Arnold Schwarzenegger videos.

"Val!" Lulu waved her hand back and forth in front of her friend's eyes. "You're in your Zeb trance again." Val's eyes were dazed, and she had lost all power of speech.

"Val!" Lulu gave her a little shake. "If you love Zeb so much, why don't you talk to him?"

Val blinked, coming out of her trance. "Not yet. I'm waiting for the perfect moment."

"Like the next solar eclipse?" Lulu joked. "It'll be dark then, so he won't see you blush."

"Don't tease me!" Val protested. "Love is complicated."

"Right." Lulu nodded. She knew a little about love. She knew that she loved her friend Val and the Angel Club, movies that made her laugh and cry at the same time, semisweet chocolate, the color red, and her dad.

The girls watched Zeb go into the Sweet Shop. "I've got to get home," Lulu stated, and they headed for Starlight Video, her dad's store.

"Uh-oh," Lulu groaned, suddenly stopping in her tracks. "Sally Jillian is coming out."

"So what?" said Val.

"Sally's been in the store every day this week. I think she's after my dad." Lulu's mom had died when Lulu was a baby. She was wild about her father and very possessive of him.

"Lulu, you are jumping to conclusions," warned Val. "Sally's your dad's accountant, remember? She has to come to the store. And she rents videos, too, like everybody else in town."

Lulu nodded. "That's true." When Sally stopped to say hi, Lulu studied her closely. She was slim and petite, with strawberry-blond hair that she wore drawn back in a tight knot. Sally never wore makeup, and she dressed in dark suits and flat shoes. It was hard to think of her as anyone's love interest.

Val glanced at her watch. "I've got to go. See you tomorrow."

"Right." Lulu nodded and ran into the store. "Dad! Guess what? I got an A+ for my movie about Angel Falls."

"Way to go!" Mr. Bliss grinned and gave Lulu a high five. Her father looked a lot like her. He had the same rumply black hair, and wore casual clothes, too. Today he was wearing a *King Kong* T-shirt and jeans. The movie *Airplane!* was blaring from the store's huge video screen.

"Are you watching that again?" Lulu teased. Harry Bliss loved comedies, the broader the better.

"It keeps me smiling," he said. "Being stuck inside a store all day can be dreary. I need all the laughs I can get."

Lulu nodded. Her dad really did work hard. She couldn't remember the last time that he'd taken a vacation.

"Help me reshelve these videos," Mr. Bliss said. Lulu often helped her dad in the store. It was always busy before dinner, when everyone rushed in to rent videos. For the next few hours, they hardly had a minute to talk at all.

Finally, Mr. Bliss closed up the shop, and they went upstairs to their apartment. It was cozy and rumpled, like them. Over the years, the two of them had picked up the furniture at flea markets. Nothing matched, which they both liked. Even the plates and glasses were all different.

"What'll it be for dinner tonight, mademoiselle?" Mr. Bliss asked Lulu.

"Caviar and cornflakes!" Lulu answered. It was a running joke they shared. Mr. Bliss was a fabulous cook, and he and Lulu often made dinner together.

"How about pumpkin tortellini? I'll teach you how to cook it. The secret is not to let the pasta cook too long."

While they set the water to boiling, Lulu told her dad about the railroad station project. "I'm going to tape it with my Minicam. It'll be great, don't you think?"

"Absolutely!" Harry Bliss agreed. "Toss in the pasta now." He gave the pot a stir as Lulu dropped in the tortellini.

"Dad, do you think I can make a good movie?"

"Of course," Mr. Bliss said confidently. "Tomorrow I'll teach you how to edit your tape. That will make your movie look professional."

"Dad, thanks." Her father was always so supportive of Lulu. For years, Lulu had been preparing the Oscar speech she'd make when she won the Best Director award. Her dad was the first person she would thank.

Between bites of tortellini and salad, Lulu chattered on about school and her friends.

After they did the dishes, Mr. Bliss stretched out on the couch. "My legs are killing me," he complained. "Standing on my feet all day is the pits."

Lulu noticed that her dad was developing crinkly wrinkles around his eyes. And his dark hair was turning salt-and-peppery.

"Don't forget to do your homework," he reminded her. "Your A+ today was terrific, but the rest of your grades haven't been too great lately."

"Right. Homework, yuck," Lulu muttered.

Before bedtime, Lulu and her dad chose the next day's movies to play in the store.

He picked *Grumpy Old Men* and *My Life as a Dog*. Lulu choose *A League of Their Own*.

"Fine. We need just one more." Mr. Bliss tapped his chin as he thought. "I'm stuck," he confessed. "Ah, well. Let's go to bed. I'll come up with another movie in the morning."

After Lulu took her shower, she settled onto her bed. "Time to call Val," she said. The two of them always talked to each other before they went to bed. "Hi! Listen," Lulu said breathlessly, "what's our math homework?"

"Pages sixty-seven and sixty-eight," Val said,

exasperated. Lulu constantly forgot. "I wish you'd remember sometimes."

"Don't be a nag," Lulu snapped. "Val—" her voice dropped to a whisper—"you were right about my jumping to conclusions about Sally Jillian and my dad. He hasn't mentioned her once."

"Didn't I tell you?" said Val confidently. "It was all in your fantastic imagination. Bye! And don't forget our Angel Club meeting tomorrow after school."

"I won't," Lulu promised. She hung up the phone and began plowing through her math.

"Hey, Lulu!" Harry Bliss knocked on her door.

"Come in," Lulu said.

Her dad stuck his head in her room. He was beaming. "I've thought of the movie I want for tomorrow."

Lulu beamed back. "Great! Which one?"

"*When Harry Met Sally . . .*" her dad said shyly. "Good night." And he closed the door.

Oh, no! When Harry Bliss met Sally Jillian! Lulu groaned. She dumped her math homework on the floor and began pacing back and forth. The only math problem Lulu could think about was: 1 Harry + 1 Sally = 1 couple!

And how would Lulu ever solve it?

2

Extra! Extra! Bora Bora!

Lulu had a hard time falling asleep that night. *Calm down,* she told herself. *It's just a movie.* But her dad had never liked romance movies—even comic ones. He always smirked at them.

She picked up the framed photo of her mother. Mrs. Bliss had a delicate face and the same almond-shaped eyes as Lulu. Her straight black hair was sleek and shimmery as she and Lulu's dad stood hand in hand on a summer day in front of Angel Falls.

Born in Japan, Lulu's mother had been an exchange student when she met Mr. Bliss. They married after knowing each other only six months. Tragically, she had died of a burst appendix four months after Lulu was born.

Lulu couldn't believe how young her father looked. He had always acted so grown-up, the strong, solid center of Lulu's life.

Sighing, Lulu gently put down that photo and picked up the one of the Angel Club. Together with her dad, Val McCall, Toby Antonio, and Rachel Summers made up Lulu's entire family.

Finally, thinking about her friends, Lulu fell asleep.

The next morning, she bounded out of bed in a better mood. At breakfast, she reminded her father about the film-editing lesson that night.

"A promise is a promise," Mr. Bliss assured her.

Later, when Lulu reached school, Lulu remembered that she'd forgotten to finish her math or do the science reading. *I hope Ms. Fisher doesn't call on me.*

Lulu hid behind a book. Sometimes it worked, sometimes not. Today she was lucky. It worked.

At lunch, Toby and Rachel both reminded Lulu of their meeting after school. "I'll remember," Lulu promised. "I wish you didn't think I was so ditsy."

When the final bell rang that day, they all hurried out the door together. Lulu smiled as Toby and Rachel walked on ahead. Rachel was the smallest girl in fifth grade and Toby the tallest. They had become best friends soon after Rachel moved to town.

Toby chattered happily as they walked. She was

very outgoing, and Rachel was shyer, though just as smart. Toby's long braid bobbed behind her. Rachel had short blond hair and bangs. It was clear from Toby's leaping around that she was talking about basketball. They both loved sports and the woods and animals.

As Lulu and Val caught up, they saw Derek Weatherby standing in front of an empty store. He wore railway overalls and was pounding away with a hammer.

"Hey, girls!" he called out. "Guess what this place is going to be?"

"Your new bookstore," Lulu answered.

Derek looked astonished. "How did you know?"

"Lulu's the first person to know anything new in town," said Val proudly.

"Because she's so nosy." Toby poked Lulu affectionately.

Toby's teasing was interrupted by a loud shriek: *"Read all about it! Extra! Extra! Read all about it!"*

"Ezra, pipe down!" Derek shouted into the open door of the store, where his pet cockatoo hopped around on a perch. "Ezra learned to say that when I sold newspapers at the train station."

"He's great." Rachel smiled. "I can't wait for your store to open. I'm going to be your best customer."

"No, *I* am," Toby insisted. She was always competitive, but in a friendly way. "Rachel and I both love mysteries, so we trade books a lot."

"Right!" said Rachel. "Twice, Toby wrote the name of the killer on the first page. That's when I wanted to kill *her*."

"Will you have lots of movie books?" Lulu asked Derek.

"Sure," he said, pleased. "If all my customers are as devoted to reading as the Angel Club, I'll earn a million dollars *per annum*. That means 'each year' in Latin."

"Hi there!" Sheriff Perkins called from his blue-and-white police car.

"Hi." Derek waved.

"Good luck with your new store. Be sure to stock a lot of spy stories. I can't get enough of them."

"I will," Derek promised.

"And how about putting in a café and coffeebar? That'll attract more customers, especially me." Sheriff Perkins patted his hefty stomach.

"Good idea." Derek nodded. "I'll think about it."

"How's the Angel Club today?" The sheriff smiled at the girls over his half-glasses, his thick white eyebrows as shaggy as usual. Even though he was six feet away, Lulu could smell his Old Spice aftershave.

"We're fine," Lulu answered, and she and Val

exchanged smiles. They'd known Sheriff Perkins since they were toddlers. Every year he played Santa. When Lulu was three, she had guessed it was him because of the Old Spice. He was as familiar a fixture in town as the angel clock.

"We're all great," Toby said, "but we've got a meeting to get to."

"Don't let me keep you angels from your business." The sheriff chuckled as the girls hurried off to Angel Stream.

"I brought some peanut butter cookies," Toby announced. Her parents owned a bakery, and she always brought the treats.

"And I brought a thermos of milk and four cups," Rachel added.

"And I have a Milky Way bar," said Lulu.

After the food was passed around, Toby volunteered to call the meeting to order. "Does anyone have any new projects for the Angel Club?"

Lulu's hand shot up. "I do. I think we should help Derek with his bookstore. He's absolutely the nicest person in town."

"I agree," added Toby. "If it weren't for Derek, I wouldn't have my dance scholarship. So does anyone have any ideas?"

"We could help him put the books on the shelves when they come in, and make sure they are in the right order," recommended Lulu. "It must be a lot like shelving videotapes."

"And we could volunteer to help customers find good books—we could suggest all of our favorites," suggested Rachel, who was the most serious reader of them all.

"Those are good ideas," said Toby, "but first, we'd better ask Derek if he wants our help."

"Yeah," seconded Val. "Maybe we'd just get underfoot. My stepfather sometimes complains about that when we're down at his newspaper office."

"Okay." Toby began to summarize. "First step is to write up a list of suggestions—I'll do that—and then ask Derek if he'd like to take us up on any. Maybe he has other ideas about how we can help."

After the Angel Club's general noises of agreement quieted down, there was a long silence while they munched their cookies.

"Any other business?" asked Toby.

"I need some advice," began Rachel in her soft voice. "Toby's been coaching me in basketball, and I was thinking of trying out for the basketball team. Do you think I should?"

"Absolutely!" said Toby. "You've improved so much."

"But am I good enough for the team?" Rachel wondered.

"Definitely," Lulu said. "And I know how to prove it. I'll shoot a video of you practicing. Then you can *see* how good you are."

"That might help." Rachel smiled. "Thanks for thinking of it, Lulu."

"Does anyone have any other official business?" Toby asked.

"Yes!" Lulu answered. "Well, maybe this isn't official business, but tomorrow I'm going to start making a movie of the railway station. I'm going to capture the whole restoration on tape."

"I have an idea," said Val. "Why don't you interview one of the workmen? That will help bring the movie to life."

"Val, that's a great idea." Lulu grinned.

"That's how my step-dad gets lots of his newspaper stories," Val added. "He interviews all kinds of people."

"Okay, that's three big projects so far," said Toby cheerfully. "Any more, or is that enough for now?" The Angel Club laughed. It did seem like an awful lot.

They spent the rest of the meeting finishing the cookies and catching up on town news.

"Sally Jillian was in the bakery doing our

accounts," Toby mentioned. "She told my mother that she's planning a trip to Bora Bora."

"Really?" Lulu's ears perked up. "Where is Bora Bora?"

"It's a tropical island near Tahiti in the South Pacific," Val said. "Mom says honeymooners love it. Her travel agency sells lots of tickets there."

"Sally did say she was getting *two* tickets." Toby looked puzzled. "Is she getting married? I didn't even think she had a boyfriend."

Lulu swallowed hard, and her heart began pounding. "Guys, I have to tell you something." Lulu took a deep breath. "I'm beginning to get worried. Sally has been hanging out at our video store lately. I think something is going on between her and my dad."

"Lulu," Val groaned. "I told you yesterday you were jumping to conclusions."

"I know. But listen to this: guess what movie Dad's playing today? *When Harry Met Sally* . . . !"

"Lulu," Toby said patiently, "it's just a movie. I agree with Val. I think you're getting carried away."

"Am I?" Lulu's eyes narrowed.

"Calm down," Toby urged. Then her expression grew wistful. "Actually, it would be nice if your dad married Rachel's mom. Then you and Rachel could be sisters. Wouldn't that be terrific?"

"Forget it." Lulu's eyes flashed angrily.

"Okay, okay!" Toby backed off. "It was just a thought. Lulu, you are getting so touchy."

"I am not." Lulu turned to Rachel. "It's nothing personal. You know I love you. And your mother is a great person. It's just that I don't want *anyone* marrying my dad."

After that, there was dead silence. Lulu was so upset, nobody knew *what* to say.

Finally, Rachel's gentle voice broke the silence. "Lulu," she said, "this might be a good time to call your guardian angel. Merrie helped me so much when *I* felt so alone in town."

"I second the motion," declared Toby. "Remember when my ballet lessons were canceled, and our bakery was in trouble? Serena was a godsend."

Val put her arm around Lulu. "I agree with Rachel and Toby. We're your friends, and the best advice we can give you is to get in touch with your angel."

Lulu shook Val's arm away. "I don't need an angel," she insisted. "I can take care of everything myself."

But could she?

Florinda, the Queen of the Angels, was not so sure.

3

A Glowing Decision

Floating on a sunbeam and holding a silver baton, Florinda was conducting a concert of the Heavenly Tambourine Band and Chorus. *I'll attend to Lulu in a moment,* she decided. *As soon as we finish this song.*

"Merrie, sing louder!" Florinda urged. "We all love your voice."

"Sure!" Merrie beamed, her red hair shimmering in the sunlight.

"Serena!" Florinda scolded. "Stop admiring your reflection in your drum, and pay attention to the song."

"Sorry!" Serena said. She smoothed an imaginary wrinkle from her golden gown and resumed pounding her drum.

"Celeste!" Florinda's beautiful brown face grew stern. "Would you kindly stop flirting with that cherub and shake your tambourine?"

"I'm not flirting," Celeste insisted. "He was teaching me a new rhythm."

"I *bet* he was," Amber teased. She was a very reliable angel who never misbehaved.

When the final notes filled the heavens, the Queen of the Angels announced, "Celeste, Amber, Merrie, and Serena, please fly to the Ruby Rotunda right away!"

There was a great flutter of wings as the cherubim and seraphim dashed off and Florinda's angels-in-training soared two hundred light years to the east, to the Angel Academy.

Celeste arrived first. She loved this room. The rounded ruby walls cast a red glow on the crystal armchairs, making her feel warm and cozy.

Celeste's ruffly green dress took up so much room, she needed a whole love seat by herself. But Celeste refused to give up even one ruffle. She ran her hand through her long black hair to comb it. She adored the really rumpled look.

"Hurry!" Florinda urged the other angels as they straggled in. "We have an emergency in Angel Corners."

As everyone took her seat, Florinda said, "Lulu Bliss needs a guardian angel right away."

"Pick me!" Amber said, raising her hand.

"No! Me!" Celeste sang.

"Hmm." Florinda flew restlessly around the room. "I'm not sure who should go. You see, Lulu doesn't know she needs an angel yet, but she's headed for trouble. While I'm thinking about it, let's have a surprise quiz in Sparkling, Shimmering, Glittering, and Glowing."

"Oh, no!" Merrie complained. "I'm so bad at surprise quizzes."

Florinda ignored her. "First, I want to review the subject matter. As you know, there are many forms of lumination. Our auras sparkle like diamonds. Just a shimmer of our wings brings peace. Overall glittering takes hard work and practice, but is especially effective. And, of course, since the beginning of time, we angels have been glowing spirits, and just a glimmer of us makes humans happy."

"That's true," Merrie claimed. "Rachel was thrilled when she saw me glittering in the woods."

"And Toby loved seeing me shimmering on her ceiling." Serena smiled.

"You were wonderful," Florinda agreed. "But we always need to polish up our skills. Let's begin with a few glowing-halo drills. Begin by thinking the happiest thoughts that you can."

Serena thought of Toby dancing *The Firebird*, and her halo shimmered a pretty, warm gold.

Merrie remembered saving a puppy's life for Rachel, and her halo glittered like a star.

Amber's halo sparkled nicely, too.

But Celeste's halo was spectacular! It glowed so brightly, the other angels had to cover their eyes with their wings.

"How did you do that?" Amber asked.

Celeste smiled dreamily. "I thought about how happy I'll be when I have a girl of my own."

"Well done," praised Florinda. "Would you please tone down your radiance now, Celeste?"

Celeste thought of Astral Algebra, and her glow quickly faded.

"Thank you.

"You all receive passing grades on the quiz," Florinda announced. "But right now, I think it's time to pick Lulu's angel."

"Lulu's adorable!" Celeste gushed. "She's curious about everything, just like me!"

"Florinda," said Amber nervously, "I hope you're not thinking of sending Celeste to Lulu. That would be a disaster."

"Actually," said Florinda, "Lulu must have an angel who is both creative and dramatic, and Celeste fits the bill perfectly."

"I'm going to earth! I'm finally going!" Celeste

leaped into the air and twirled around, beaming so brightly, the other angels had to shield their eyes once again.

"Please, a little self-control," Florinda warned. "You mustn't light up that brightly on earth. It's too much for mere humans to take."

"I'm sorry." Celeste dimmed again.

"Now, listen closely," said Florinda. "Lulu Bliss believes that she is losing her father's love. We all know that love is the most important thing in the world. None of us can live without it. Lulu is going through a frightening time."

"I'll stay close to her," Celeste promised.

"There's one serious complication." Florinda sighed. "Remember, Lulu Bliss has not asked for an angel. She's very independent, and she thinks she can handle everything herself."

"Don't worry," Celeste said confidently. "When Lulu gets to know me, I'm sure she'll let me help her."

"That's *if* she gets to know you," Florinda said, looking worried. "We'll hope for the best. Now, however, before you fly away, Celeste, let's review the Angelic Rules together."

"I'll start," Merrie volunteered. "Rule One: You can turn into anything you like on earth. I suggest birds. It's fun being quick and teeny."

"Rule Two," said Serena. "Angels are very surprising, so proceed slowly. I wrote Toby lots of notes before I appeared."

"Rule Three," said Amber. "Remember, nobody on earth can see you except your girl."

"And Rule Four," said Florinda firmly, "is that you do not show yourself to Lulu until she asks for you. Of course, this is the most important rule to remember right now. Lulu doesn't know she needs you. You will have to wait for her."

Celeste sighed. "That may take a long time. So while I'm waiting, I'll explore the town and watch the movies at Starlight Video. I'll get a close look at Zeb Burgess, too. He's soooo dreamy."

"Just keep an eye and an ear open for Lulu's call, Celeste. I am sending you to Lulu, not to Zeb Burgess!" said Florinda sternly, but with a light in her eye.

"Come here." Florinda enveloped Celeste in her warm silver wings. "I want to give you a blessing before you leave." Very softly, the Queen of the Angels crooned, "May your visit to Lulu Bliss bring her strength and remind her how very much she is loved."

"Amen," sang Serena, Amber, and Merrie.

Then Celeste flew off to make her brilliant first visit to earth.

CHAPTER

4

Endangered!

That night, at dinner, Lulu didn't have much of an appetite. She picked at her plate of fried chicken and mashed potatoes. Usually, it was her favorite meal.

Mr. Bliss seemed distracted, too. He was reading *Money* magazine as he ate.

"Are we running out of money?" Lulu asked.

"Um . . . no," Mr. Bliss answered, not looking up from his reading.

"How about tomorrow's movies for the store?" Lulu said, trying to get her dad's attention. "We haven't picked them yet."

"Later," he said, still deep in his magazine.

"Dad!" Lulu said loudly. "You were supposed to

teach me how to edit videotape tonight, remember?"

Harry Bliss put the magazine down and shook his head. "I can't tonight, Lulu. I forgot that I have to work on our financial records tonight."

"But you promised," Lulu said angrily. "How can I make my movie of the railway station if I can't edit?"

"I'll do it another time," Mr. Bliss said testily. "Sally Jillian is coming over first thing in the morning to help with financial planning. She's a whiz at it."

"Oh, really?" Lulu's face flushed, but her dad didn't notice. "Does she help you a lot?" she asked more loudly than she meant to.

"Lately she has." Mr. Bliss smiled. "Sally's terrific at plotting the future."

"I'll bet she is," Lulu muttered to herself.

Mr. Bliss whistled a tune as he scrubbed the frying pan. "I'll teach you film editing soon, Lulu, I promise. But don't wait for me. Just begin shooting."

I know someone I want to shoot, Lulu thought as she went to her room later. *I'm not jumping to conclusions. This Sally stuff is getting serious!*

Lulu grabbed her Minicam and stuck in a new videocassette for tomorrow's shooting. She cleaned the lens carefully and tucked the Minicam into its protective case. Lulu might be careless with other things, but never with her camera.

Later, Mr. Bliss knocked on Lulu's door to say good night. "Hey, kiddo! We forgot to pick the films for tomorrow."

"You do it," Lulu murmured from under her covers. "I'm too tired." What she really meant was *I don't want to, not until you stop thinking about Sally Jillian!*

"Okay. Sweet dreams, mademoiselle." Mr. Bliss blew Lulu a kiss.

When he was gone, Lulu phoned Val.

"Guess what?" Val sounded excited. "I came up with the greatest idea for extra credit in science. I'm building a miniature rain forest for my science proj—"

"Fine, fine!" Lulu interrupted. "Listen, Val, I have to tell you the latest about my father. Sally is coming over tomorrow to go over his financial future. Doesn't that sound awful?"

"Finances are Sally's job," said Val, annoyed. "I keep telling you that."

"But Dad whistled as he did the dishes, Val. He never whistles."

Val groaned. "You are driving yourself—and me—crazy! Why don't you just come right out and ask your dad if he's interested in Sally?"

"I can't," Lulu said softly. "I'm afraid of the answer."

"Really? I didn't think you were afraid of *anything*, Lulu."

"Well, I am!" Lulu blurted. "Look, I've got to hang up. Good night!" She slammed down the phone before Val could say another word.

Lulu paced around her room. The thought of anyone coming between her and her dad tied her stomach in knots.

She tried to calm herself down by reading her favorite book, *Feature Filmmaking at Used-Car Prices,* but it was no use. Lulu kept reading the same page over and over. Finally, she turned off the light and got into bed.

But she just tossed and turned. She tried punching her pillow a few times to make it more comfy, but it was no use. Then she put on the radio, but the noisy music was no help, so she turned it off.

"I wish my wind chimes would play," she sighed. "They might help me fall asleep."

Instantly, a soft tinkling sound came from the wind chimes in the tree outside Lulu's window. Her dad had given them to Lulu when she was five and afraid of the dark. "When you hear their song," he had assured her, "it will remind you that I'm always nearby."

Tonight the chimes sounded more musical than

usual. They had a rich, mellow tone, as if a lovely harp were playing.

Lulu threw back the covers and went over to the window. The long, silvery chimes were glowing brightly. "There must be a full moon tonight," Lulu whispered. But there wasn't. The sky was covered with clouds.

"That's odd," Lulu said. She noticed that the leaves in the tree were perfectly still.

There wasn't the slightest breeze. So why were the wind chimes ringing?

Lulu was puzzled. She pondered it while she got back into bed.

The sweet song of the wind chimes comforted and calmed Lulu, and she quickly fell asleep.

The next morning, Lulu woke up to a loud thumping.

"What's going on?" she wondered. She put on her robe and went out into the hallway.

"Hi!" Mr. Bliss was there, doing jumping jacks in his Rocky Balboa T-shirt and sweatpants. "Sorry I woke you!" he panted. "I've decided to start exercising." He patted his stomach. "I've been getting a little flabby."

"Oh? I didn't notice," Lulu muttered.

"I'm thinking of growing a mustache, too," Mr. Bliss said, his face flushing red. "Do you think it will make me better-looking?"

Lulu swallowed hard. These were terrible signs! "Dad," Lulu blurted out. "Don't change a thing! I love you just the way you are!"

"And Mister Rogers and I love *you* just the way *you* are," her dad teased. "But nevertheless, there's always room for improvement."

Lulu made a face and went to get dressed.

She threw on a pink shirt and a leopard-print vest, and completed the outfit with baggy blue jeans, a gold sock, a blue sock, and sneakers.

After a quick breakfast alone—her dad was in the shower—Lulu packed up for school. She noticed the films Mr. Bliss had picked for the store: *Splash, The Little Mermaid,* and *South Pacific.*

Lulu tried not to think about that as she set off for school. Passing the railroad station, she saw the workmen sitting against the building, eating their breakfast of coffee and bagels.

I'll take a few quick shots of the station now, she decided, *while the bricks are still dirty. Then I'll have a neat before-and-after movie.* Lulu walked around the station, filming all sides of it.

Then she aimed her Minicam at the workmen, still sipping coffee. As Lulu zoomed in, she noticed that one of the men wore one black sock and one brown.

"Hey, you're just like me!" Lulu pointed at her feet. "You don't wear matching socks."

The man nodded and then looked away. Lulu continued walking down the street.

"Good morning!" Sally Jillian was suddenly there, walking toward Lulu. She was wearing bright pink lipstick, and her hair wasn't drawn back into a knot. She was wearing it down in soft curls. Lulu almost didn't recognize her.

"Hullo." Lulu nodded curtly at Sally and then broke into a run. She kept on running all the way to school. When she saw Val, she was eager to tell her the latest awful clues.

But Val began talking first. "Did you do the reading homework? There were terrific photos of koalas and puffins."

"I forgot," Lulu admitted. She wanted to talk to Val more, but the school bell rang. As she sat down, Lulu said, "I hope Ms. Fisher doesn't call on me."

But this time, she did.

"Lulu Bliss." Ms. Fisher fixed her in a steady gaze. "Can you tell me one place where the animals are endangered?"

"Bora Bora?" Lulu blurted.

"Really?" Ms. Fisher replied. "What animal were you thinking of?"

"Um . . . Free Willy? Wasn't he a killer whale or something?"

"That's exactly what he was," Ms. Fisher replied.

"But killer whales weren't in your reading assignment. Lulu, did you read it at all?"

"Um . . . no," Lulu confessed.

"Lulu only knows animals in movies," Felicia McWithers called out. "Ask her about *A Fish Called Wanda* or *Groundhog Day.*"

"That will do!" Ms. Fisher glared at Felicia. "Lulu, you're a bright girl, but you are simply not applying yourself."

"I'll try harder," Lulu promised, and she really meant it.

At the end of class, the teacher announced, "Tomorrow's reading will be chapter seven on the rain forest. Are you writing this down, Lulu?"

"Yes!" She nodded, scribbling.

Val rushed over to Lulu's desk the second the bell rang. "Come over to my house later, and I'll help you with the homework."

"I can do it myself," Lulu insisted.

Then the whole Angel Club headed for Toby's house. Lulu had her camera with her to videotape Rachel's basketball practice.

When they passed Derek's soon-to-be bookstore, his cockatoo was shrieking, *"Read all about it! Read all about it!"*

Rachel giggled. "That's a perfect thing to say in a bookstore, isn't it?"

"Hey, girls," Derek said proudly, "I just got my first special order. Lulu's dad wants a travel book called *Tropical Island Paradises*. "

Lulu gulped. "Oh, no!"

"What's the matter?" Derek asked.

"Oh, nothing," Val answered for Lulu.

Just then Toby stepped forward with the Angel Club's list of ways to help Derek fix up his store. "We'd like to help you out, Derek, if you don't mind the help of amateurs."

"You're all angels! I can use all the help I can get. Let me look this over and get back to you. Thanks." He was incredibly pleased.

"See you, then," said Toby.

As they continued on, Val whispered to Lulu, "Will you please calm down? Your dad's always been a great reader. I'm sure it's just a coincidence that Bora Bora, where Sally Jillian is going, is a tropical island paradise."

"You're making it worse!" Lulu glared at her friend. "Will you please shut up?"

"Okay, I'm sorry!" Val looked hurt.

Toby asked Lulu angrily, "When will you listen to us and ask your angel for help? I'm starting to worry about you."

"I'm fine!" Lulu insisted. "I keep telling you, I don't need any angel."

"Okay, let's change the subject," said Val. She knew it was no use arguing with Lulu when she got really stubborn. "Will you come over later and help me design my rain forest? You always have such great ideas."

"Sure, sure," Lulu promised.

"Thanks," Val said gratefully. "I'm making models of endangered species. The monkeys are so cute. Of course, they're not as cute as Zeb, but pretty close."

Lulu nodded, but she wasn't thinking of monkeys. Her mind was on one particular endangered creature: her dad.

5

Stormy Weather

When Lulu and her friends reached Toby's house, Rachel and Toby rushed upstairs, above the bakery, to change their clothes.

Soon Rachel returned, wearing a blue sweatshirt and drawstring pants. Toby wore her T-shirt that proudly proclaimed her a member of the ANGEL CORNERS MIDDLE SCHOOL BASKETBALL TEAM.

"Let me warm up before you start filming," Rachel said to Lulu. She and Toby did some stretches, and Rachel practiced tossing baskets from the free-throw line.

Michael Jordan, Toby's cat, watched from the shade of the oak tree.

"Okay," Toby said impatiently. "You're warmed

up. Let's start playing some one-on-one. Lulu, start shooting whenever you're ready."

"Gotcha!" Lulu loved being behind the camera. It made her feel in charge. She zoomed in on Rachel's footwork, which was very smooth.

It was great the way Rachel dodged and twisted and got around Toby, who was so much taller.

"Way to go," praised Toby, panting. "I can hardly get a shot off."

In fact, Toby got so frustrated, she aimed the ball wildly, and it bounced out into the street.

"I'll get it," Val offered, but Sheriff Perkins was suddenly there, crossing the street. He set down a bag of groceries and grabbed the ball.

"Thanks!" Rachel caught the ball as he tossed it back.

"Whew! Am I out of shape!" Sheriff Perkins gasped. "It's all this pepperoni." He pointed at a long sausage sticking out of his grocery bag. "Mrs. Perkins and I love to cook. She especially loves pepperoni pizza, and I'm wild about her, so I make it just for her. I prefer straight mushroom and olive, which she makes just for me!"

Lulu and the others smiled at the love-smitten sheriff.

"See you." He waved and headed home.

"Do we have enough shots of Rachel?" Toby asked Lulu.

"It's a wrap," said Lulu.

"Then let's watch the tape while we have a snack."

Toby dashed into her parents' bakery and then met the Angel Club in the family's den with a plate of fat-free cookies her mother had created and four glasses of milk. The girls settled down on the huge couch as Lulu slipped the tape into the VCR. Toby grabbed the remote and turned it on.

Rachel leaned forward, spellbound. When she saw how well she'd handled Toby's height advantage, a smile lit up her face. And as she watched her free-throw form, she positively beamed.

"Hey, I'm *good*!" Rachel shouted.

"That's what I've been trying to tell you." Toby rolled her eyes.

"I guess I had to see myself from the outside, you know?" said Rachel.

"Right." Lulu nodded. "I'll bring my Minicam to your tryout, too, and catch your expression when you make the team. And then the Angel Club can go to the Sweet Shop to celebrate."

"Neat idea." Toby smiled. "I've already made up a cheer:

"RACHEL! RACHEL! CAN'T BE BEAT!

WATCH HER SLAM-DUNK!

SHE IS NEAT."

"I'll be the loudest cheerer," Lulu vowed. "But

right now, I have to go work on my movie at the railway station."

"Hey," Val said. "You promised to come and help me with my rain forest, remember?"

"I can't." Lulu shook her head. "I have to film every day after school, and the light is fading."

"But I need your help." Val's eyes looked pained. "And you promised."

"I don't remember promising," Lulu said curtly, and she walked away. Lulu felt a pang of guilt, but she brushed the feeling aside.

When she reached the railway station, she unpacked her camera. The workmen were standing on a scaffold, sandblasting the top of the building. They made a terrible racket.

Sand flew into Lulu's nose and eyes as she chose her long shots, close-ups, pans, and angles, but she protected her camera as best she could. She stopped now and then to wipe off her lens.

When she was done, Lulu put away her Minicam. Just then, the railway station door opened, and Sally Jillian walked out with Mr. Sabin, the stationmaster. "I'm so glad you've asked me to do your accounts," Sally was saying. "I can really use the work."

Lulu noticed that Sally was wearing makeup again, and her hair looked as if she'd gotten a permanent. She wore a nice-fitting pantsuit and high heels, too, instead of flats.

"Hi, Lulu." Sally smiled warmly, revealing a dimple. "Your dad said you were filming the restoration. That's a terrific idea."

"*I* think so," Lulu replied coldly. Then she ran over to the workmen, who were beginning to climb down from the scaffold. "I'd like to interview one of you on camera," she said. She chose the man who wore socks that didn't match. Today he had on one blue and one green.

"Do you mind?"

"I guess not," he said. The tall, broad man did not take off his protective mask and gloves.

"Great! You can keep your mask on—it'll make a neat shot."

"Okay." The man laughed a bit nervously.

"Um . . . what's your name?"

"Chet Harris." Lulu closed in on his mask, then moved back for a full shot.

"Can you tell me what other buildings you've done?"

The man shrugged. "Lots of them."

Lulu persisted. "Like what?"

He thought for a moment. "Um . . . Grand Central Station in New York City."

"Wow! That place is incredible!" Lulu was

impressed. Chet Harris nodded and took off one of his gloves. His hands were huge, and Lulu went in for another close-up.

"Did you use the same equipment there?"

"Sure. But we had more workmen . . . about a hundred. Hey, kid, I don't have all night. Why don't you talk to one of the other guys."

Chet Harris turned and quickly disappeared around the corner of the station.

Darn it. Lulu felt frustrated. But just then the angel clock struck six. "Ooops!" she blurted. "I have to go, too. It's almost time for dinner. Dad will be worried."

By the time she reached her block, Starlight Video was closed for the night. Lulu slid her key into the lock on the apartment door. Through the opened doorway she called out, "Hi, Dad." But nobody answered. The house was dark, too.

"Dad?" Lulu called again. She went into the kitchen and turned on the light. There was a note on the refrigerator door: *Lulu! I had a meeting to go to. Make yourself a salad and don't wait up for me. I'll be home late. Dad.*

Lulu gulped. Her dad rarely went out at night. "He's seeing Sally!" Lulu shouted. "I just know it!" Her voice sounded loud and angry in the empty apartment.

She had absolutely no appetite for dinner. Besides, it was no fun to eat alone.

I guess I'll look at my film and see how it's coming, Lulu decided. She popped the videocassette into the VCR and sat down to watch it in her dad's leather chair.

Hmm. Not bad. Lulu smiled. *The sandblasting shots are clear. But I have to catch more of that Chet guy on camera tomorrow, and without his mask.*

Lulu paced forlornly around the apartment. It was odd how it could feel so different when she was the only one home.

As she heard her footsteps echoing in the empty apartment, Lulu became angrier and angrier. *Dad should've left me a note saying where he went. What if there's an emergency or something?*

Lulu tried to distract herself by reading her homework, but she kept wondering where her father was. *There's only one way to find out,* she decided. She grabbed a flashlight. *I'll go to Sally's house and see if he's there.*

As Lulu left the apartment, she tried not to think about what she would say if she *did* find her father there. She just kept on walking, almost in a daze of single-mindedness.

She passed house after house of families eating dinner together. Lulu could almost hear the clink of silverware in the heavy evening air. The streets were deserted. Only Lulu seemed to be outside.

After a twenty-minute walk, Lulu reached Sally's house. Lighting her way with the flashlight, she walked up the sidewalk to Sally's front door.

The house was completely dark. *Should I ring the doorbell?* Lulu wondered.

She took a deep breath and rang the bell. Nobody answered.

"There's no one home," Lulu said, relieved. "Dad isn't here."

Suddenly Lulu began to feel very alone, standing on Sally's darkened doorstep. A few raindrops began to fall. As she headed back home, the drops grew fatter and came down more frequently.

Lulu could see lightning in the distance. She shivered and walked faster. Lulu hated thunderstorms. Indoors—home—was the coziest place to be, and she couldn't wait to get there.

Lulu began to run, but the storm was faster. It soon reached her, thundering, flashing, and soaking her thoroughly.

Finally, she reached her apartment and rushed inside. "Dad?" she called. But he still wasn't home.

Lulu stripped off her wet clothes and put on a warm robe. As she did, a powerful streak of lightning lit up the night. Thunder followed.

Then, suddenly, all the lights went off!

Lulu ran to her bed and scrunched under the covers. The lightning and thunder were getting so close!

She squinched her eyes shut, but she could still see flashes of lightning. Then the loudest thunderclap she had ever heard shook the entire house!

"Please, somebody, help!" Lulu cried. "I need my guardian angel! Would you please, please come right now?"

Instantly, the lightning flashes faded, and a radiant pink light filled the room. The glow shimmered warmly, growing brighter and brighter.

"I am here!" crooned a soft, lilting voice. "Everything will be all right now, Lulu. Sit up and open your eyes."

Lulu took a long, deep breath and did just that.

Her eyes took a moment to become adjusted to the glow.

Then, gazing up, Lulu saw her: right in front of the movie poster of *Miracle on 34th Street* was her guardian angel!

CHAPTER

6

I Can Take Care of Myself

"Whoo!" Lulu stared at Celeste, quite amazed. Her angel's light was so intense, it lit up the entire room.

"I'm the brightest angel in my class!" Celeste bragged. She flew over to Lulu and then slowly floated down, the green ruffles in her dress fluttering. "My name is Celeste," the angel said in a sweet, husky voice. She landed on the bed so lightly that she made not the slightest dent in the bedspread.

"I couldn't come until you called me," Celeste reminded Lulu as she gently stroked her forehead.

"I know," Lulu said, nodding. "I'm so glad you came. You know, it was sort of an accident, my asking for you. It just sort of popped out."

"Well, I'm glad it did," Celeste said cheerfully. "Angels love to be needed. Why don't you settle back into bed? I'll keep you company until the storm is over."

"My room looks so beautiful in your light!" Lulu's bedroom walls reflected Celeste's shimmer. "Your dress is pretty, too, and your hair." Lulu couldn't stop complimenting her angel.

"Thank you!" Celeste said gratefully. "Now, can I help you with anything else besides keeping you company until the storm settles down? I would really like to help you, if you will let me."

"I don't think so," Lulu said.

"Really?" Celeste's face filled with surprise. "How about your dad and Sally? Haven't they been on your mind?"

Lulu's eyes narrowed. "I can take care of them myself."

"Hmm," Celeste said softly. "And what about Val? You two don't seem to be getting along well lately."

"Oh, we'll work that out," Lulu said breezily.

Celeste's face grew sad, and the light in the room dimmed. "How about school?" she asked hopefully.

"School is fine," Lulu insisted. "I just have to study more, that's all."

Celeste gave up. "All right. Let's talk about movies, then."

That gave Lulu an incredible idea. She grabbed her Minicam and aimed it at Celeste. "I'm going to be the first one on earth to film an angel!"

Celeste giggled. "That's impossible. No film on earth is fast enough to capture an angel."

"Really?" Lulu was so disappointed.

"I'm afraid so," said Celeste. "I'd love to be in a movie! I've been watching a lot at your dad's store. Kevin Costner is dreamy, isn't he? So is Keanu Reeves."

Lulu smiled. "Don't tell me you're as boy-crazy as Val."

Celeste flushed crimson. "I'm an angel! I love everybody."

"Sure, sure," Lulu teased.

Celeste leaped away, trying to hide her blush, and changed the subject. "How did you like the way I played your wind chimes? I got a B+ in Heavenly Music class."

"So that was you," Lulu crooned. "It was lovely." She hugged her pillow and yawned.

"Of course that was me." Celeste landed on the bed again. "I'm here at your command!" She looked at Lulu hopefully.

"Um. Hmm." Lulu closed her eyes. "I'm getting awfully drowsy."

And in a moment, she was asleep.

Celeste stroked Lulu's rumpled hair. "I want so much to help you, if only you would let me."

Celeste was so troubled, she flew to the Angel Academy to seek Florinda's advice.

Celeste arrived at the Aquamarine Auditorium in the middle of a lecture on Angelology.

Florinda waved to Celeste. "Come up to the stage, dear. You can be Exhibit A in my demonstration."

"A for angel?" Celeste asked.

"Correct. You have all been watching Celeste comfort Lulu while a thunderstorm raged. Wasn't she splendid! I think she deserves a great round of applause."

Everyone clapped, and two cherubim struck their triangles to add to the compliments.

"Celeste's first visit to earth is off to a good start," Florinda proclaimed. "People often become fearful when there are storms. But if they could see what I'm going to show you right now, they wouldn't worry so much."

Florinda waved her arm in the air, and the floor of the auditorium became transparent. Far below, the blue earth sparkled. They could all see every stream and hill, every village and city, on the planet.

Hovering over all of them were glowing angels.

Florinda beamed. "Every inch of earth is watched over by an angel. Each blade of grass has an angel whispering to it, "Grow! Grow!"

The angels-in-training were impressed.

"Tell us more," begged Amber.

"I intend to," Florinda said. "Praxil is the name of the angel who watches over the second hour of the night."

Merrie waved at Praxil, who waved back.

"Merrie, please behave yourself," Florinda scolded. "Pilalel is the name of the angel who guards the gates of the west wind."

"Pilalel. That sounds like a poem," Serena said. She wrote the name down on her silver slate with crystal chalk. The chalk was wonderful; it never squeaked.

"And did you know," Florinda continued, "that every autumn day has its own angel? Today's angel is Tarquam."

Tarquam was orange and gold and red, like autumn itself.

"Spell it, please," called out Amber.

"T-A-R-Q-U-A-M. Now—"

A voice from the back of the auditorium interrupted Florinda. "Excuse me," a young male angel said, "but if every blade of grass, every hour, and all the winds are watched over by angels, why is there so much trouble on earth?"

"A very good question, which I will take up at our next lesson. For now, let me remind you that angels rely on humans to accept them and their work. For instance, Lulu will have to accept Celeste before she can benefit from her angel's work."

When Florinda dismissed the class, Celeste said, "I need to talk to you. You were right: Lulu doesn't seem to want me to help her."

"But she did call you during the thunderstorm," said Florinda. "You will just have to maintain your angelic patience a while longer."

Celeste nodded. "I'm certainly seeing a lot of movies while I'm waiting. I love to watch the actresses. It must be wonderful to be a star!"

"You already *are* one," Florinda assured her.

Celeste beamed. "Florinda, you always make me feel better."

"That's *my* angelic job." The Queen of the Angels smiled.

As Celeste flew back to the sleeping town of Angel Corners, the other angels-in-training continued their studies by starlight.

That isn't the least bit surprising. Because while humans are asleep, angels are *always* working.

7

One Rain Forest,
Coming Up!

Lulu woke up more rested than she'd felt in weeks. Her dad was already in the kitchen, frying French toast. "I'm awfully sorry about last night," he said quickly. "I should have warned you that I had to go out. I tried to call, but the telephone was busy."

"So where were you?" Lulu asked. She knew he had not called. There had been no message on the answering machine, and she hadn't heard the phone ring.

"Um . . . I was . . ." her dad stammered. He blushed. "A friend had kind of an . . . emergency . . . kind of. . . ."

It was clear that he was lying. Mr. Bliss always

gave himself away by blinking fast when he tried to lie.

"What friend?" Lulu persisted.

"Whoops! Guess what?" Mr. Bliss stood up. "We've run out of maple syrup. I'll go to the grocery and get some."

And before Lulu could say another word, he had dashed out the door.

Lulu's heart beat like a drum. *Dad ran out of the house like a scared rabbit. He doesn't want to tell me what he's up to, so he must be seeing Sally!*

Lulu was angrier than she'd ever been in her life. She rushed to her room and grabbed her Minicam.

"I know how to break up this romance right away!" she said out loud. "I'll watch Sally like a hawk. I'll catch her doing something awful, and when she does, I'll have my camera ready. When Dad sees just how mean and miserable she can be, he'll dump her for sure. I just have to catch her."

Lulu ran out of the apartment. *Dad can have breakfast by himself. Let him see how awful it is to eat alone.*

At the railroad station, commuters were catching the early train. Chet and the other workmen were sitting down against the building, eating their breakfast in the morning sun.

"How about a quick interview?" Lulu asked Chet.

"Not now." He shook his head. "Can't I eat my bagel in peace?"

Sheriff Perkins came over, his Old Spice overpowering the aroma of fresh coffee. "Lulu," he warned. "Not everyone wants to be a movie star, you know."

"Why not?" she asked.

"Because it invades their privacy."

"Even when you're filming something for a good cause? Like the renovation?" she asked. *Or showing Sally Jillian at her worst,* she thought.

"Even then. You need the subject's permission," explained the sheriff.

"Thanks for the info, Sheriff," said Lulu. *Whew,* she thought, *this might be trickier than I thought.*

Lulu rushed off toward school. On her way, she saw Derek washing the window of his new bookstore.

"Sunny day! High in the seventies!" shrieked his cockatoo from a perch near the open door.

Lulu stopped to chat. "Ezra's memorized the weather forecast now."

"That's right." Derek nodded. "Hey, aren't you out early this morning, Lulu?"

"Yeah."

"Come and take a look at my cappuccino machine. Sheriff Perkins came up with that idea, remember? I'm sure it will lure more customers."

As Derek poured himself a cup, Lulu suddenly felt hungry.

"Have you had your breakfast yet?" Derek seemed to be reading her mind. "How about a slice of banana bread?"

"All right. Thanks!" Lulu sat on a huge box of books and gobbled up the bread.

"There's milk, too." Derek poured some into a mug.

"You're so nice." Lulu smiled. "I'm going to tell everyone in the world to come and buy books here."

"I'll need every customer I can get," Derek answered. "I've sunk my last dime into this place."

Lulu finished the banana bread and gulped down her milk. "I'd better go."

"See you!" Derek said.

When Lulu reached school and sat down, she got a sinking feeling. *I forgot to do my homework again! What was it? Lots of rain-forest stuff.*

She glanced over at Val's desk, but Val wouldn't return her gaze. She looked angry. *I forgot to call Val, too.* Lulu realized. *It's the first night I've missed in years.*

Lulu noticed Val's rain-forest project in a glass terrarium by the window. It looked awfully pathetic. Val had been right when she had said she needed Lulu's help badly.

"Good morning," Ms. Fisher said briskly. "We'll

start the day with a pop quiz on the rain forest."

Lulu swallowed hard. "Uh-oh."

"Felicia McWithers," the teacher began. "Can you name the country with the largest rain forest in the world?"

Felicia jingled her bracelets nervously. "Um . . . Palm Beach? My mother goes there a lot."

"That is not correct." Ms. Fisher wrote F in her grade book next to Felicia's name.

"Sylvie Sawyer, do you know the answer?" Ms. Fisher asked.

"Yes. Brazil," said Sylvie.

"Right! Sylvie gets an A."

Sylvie's friend Andrea gave her a thumbs-up sign.

"Now, name three rain-forest animals that are endangered. Lulu Bliss?"

Lulu's mind was a total blank. "Um . . ." she said. "Uh . . ." An awful silence filled the room.

Suddenly Jimmy Nordstrom shouted, "Ms. Fisher! Look at Val's rain forest. Something's moving in there."

Everyone swiveled in their seats to see. Things *were* moving! Green buds were growing up from the soil, opening into tiny palm trees! Dark monkeys appeared in the trees and squealed as they leaped from branch to branch. Sloths, dangling upside down, woke up and opened their eyes.

"What's going on?" Ms. Fisher rushed to Val's science project, and the entire class followed her.

"I know," shouted Sam Eisenstein. "Val filled the tank with those paper things you order from comic books—the ones that grow when you add water."

"Well, whatever she did, Val gets an A+ today," Ms. Fisher announced.

Val began explaining that she was as surprised as everyone else, but nobody was paying attention to her.

"Well, Miss Movie Director," Celeste whispered in Lulu's ear. "How do you like the special effects I just created?"

Lulu almost jumped out of her skin. "*You* did that?"

"Of course I did! I couldn't hover around and watch you get an F, could I? I don't approve of pop quizzes—unless they're in Shimmering and Glittering. See you!" Celeste vanished.

I've got to tell the Angel Club about Celeste right now, Lulu decided.

"Val! Toby! Rachel!" Lulu whispered loudly. "Come here!" Lulu was sure Ms. Fisher wouldn't notice them. She was riveted on the rain forest, using her pointer as she named every animal.

"What's wrong?" Rachel asked as the Angel Club gathered.

"Nothing," Lulu said, smiling. "I wanted to tell you that my guardian angel came. Her name is Celeste, and she's the one who just made the rain forest grow."

"That means you called her!" Toby patted Lulu on the back. "Way to go!"

Lulu nodded. "Well, I sort of called her. Last night."

"I'm so glad," Val said sincerely. "Not just because she just helped me get an A, but because I'm worried about us. Lulu, we two have been fighting so much. Last night, we didn't say good night to each other. And this morning, I was so mad, I didn't even want to look at you."

"I know," Lulu said. "But things will be fine from now on, I promise."

"Class, come to order." Ms. Fisher was walking back to her desk. Everyone sat down again. "That was splendid, Val. Thank you for a wonderful demonstration."

"Lulu Bliss," said Ms. Fisher as she turned her gaze on her, "don't think I didn't notice that you did not study last night. You are receiving an F for today."

"Oh, no!" Lulu groaned.

"And if this happens one more time, I'm sending a note home to your father. Do you understand?"

"Yes," Lulu said softly. *Some help my guardian*

angel is! she thought. *Even though she does great special effects!*

At that moment, Celeste heard Florinda summoning her to the Crystal Classroom.

"Young angel," Florinda began sternly, "you, too, are getting an F today."

"Me?" Celeste's blue eyes went wide. "What's wrong? I don't understand."

"You are interfering in Lulu's schoolwork. Celeste, you know very well that all of us—Lulu included—must work at our studies. How will Lulu accomplish anything if you always rescue her? She needs to learn things herself."

"That's right," agreed Amber. "If you had sent me, Florinda, I would have set a better example for Lulu."

"Teacher's pet," hissed Celeste.

"From now on," instructed Florinda, "you must help Lulu—comfort, encourage, and guard her—but not interfere with her responsibilities."

"All right," Celeste said.

"Come here, dear." Florinda drew her close for a hug, crushing some of Celeste's ruffles. "Now, don't be discouraged. I warned you that Lulu is a handful."

"That's for sure." Celeste nodded.

Then she hurried back to earth.

CHAPTER

8

Take One

When Lulu got home from school, she grabbed her science book right away. She couldn't bear the thought of Ms. Fisher writing her dad a note. He would flip if that happened.

It took a whole hour, but Lulu managed to catch up on all her reading. She even felt a little proud of herself when she finished.

That night, Harry Bliss showed up at dinner with his rumpled hair slicked down with gel and neatly combed.

And he had changed his usual T-shirt and jeans for a blue velour sweater and gray slacks.

He noticed Lulu's look of surprise. "I got tired of dressing like a slob," Mr. Bliss explained. "And I've been in a rut for years. I never go anywhere, and I hardly ever see friends outside the store. That's not healthy, Lulu, for me or for you."

"Why not?" said Lulu quickly. "I like our rut."

Her dad shook his head. "Lulu, you're the first one to complain when life is boring. You're wild about surprises, remember?"

"Some surprises are better than others," Lulu responded.

Mr. Bliss looked at Lulu warmly. "That's true. In fact, there is something I have been wanting to tell you."

Lulu gulped. "My stomach hurts," she lied, and stood up. "Tell me another time."

Mr. Bliss looked perplexed. "Can I get you some Pepto-Bismol?"

"I'll get it myself!" Lulu yelled over her shoulder as she ran to her room.

It was obvious. Her dad was going to tell her about Sally. But Lulu wouldn't listen. "I won't share him with anyone," she declared. "I absolutely won't."

Lulu heard a small voice. "Lulu, please let me help you." It was Celeste.

Lulu shook her head. "I can take care of this myself, but thanks anyway."

When Val phoned to say good night, she reminded Lulu about Rachel's basketball tryout the next day. "You promised to bring your Minicam, remember? You said you would shoot Rachel and get her on camera when she makes the team—I mean, if she makes the team."

"Yeah, I know," Lulu answered. "Listen, I have to tell you the latest about my dad." And she repeated their whole conversation.

"Hmm," Val said, and was quiet for a moment. Then she asked, "Lulu, don't you think your father deserves some fun in his life? All he does is work, and he's so good to you. Doesn't he have the right to have a girlfriend?"

"No!" said Lulu stubbornly. Then she hung up and did some more homework to distract herself from thoughts of her dad. She thought she did a pretty good job.

The next morning, Lulu rushed through breakfast. She didn't want to talk to her dad until she caught Sally on tape doing something awful. That would convince her father that she was right about Sally and that he was wrong.

"Are you feeling better?" Mr. Bliss asked, looking worried.

"Yeah, yeah," said Lulu, and rushed off to school.

When Ms. Fisher called on her in science, Lulu knew all the answers.

"Good for you." Ms. Fisher smiled.

It was nice to be smiled at by her teacher for a change. Lulu made sure to write down the next day's assignments carefully.

But the minute the last bell rang, Lulu was out the door ahead of everyone else in class.

"Hey, Lulu!" she heard Rachel call, but she ignored her. *I've got to catch Sally on tape,* she told herself.

Lulu got lucky right away. She taped Sally walking down Main Street, heading for Val's mother's travel agency. She carried a huge purse, but there didn't seem to be much in it.

Aha! She's buying her tickets to Bora Bora, Lulu decided. *I can't follow her inside, though. I'll wait until she comes out.*

Lulu hovered in a nearby doorway, with her camera on her shoulder.

"What are you up to, young lady?" It was Sheriff Perkins.

"Uh, nothing."

"Um. Hmm. Can I see your camera, Lulu?" Sheriff Perkins asked.

She handed it to him.

He turned it on and shot a few frames of Lulu standing in the doorway.

"Why did you do that?" she asked. "You wasted some film."

"No, I didn't," Sheriff Perkins said. "When you have a moment, look at yourself on that tape. You might discover something interesting."

"What?" Lulu couldn't imagine.

"You'll see." He smiled. "In the meantime, there's something I want to remind you about. Remember what I said about badgering folks the other day? If you keep after somebody, that's called stalking, and it's a crime."

"Really?" Lulu's face went pink. "I would never do that."

"I'm glad to hear it." Sheriff Perkins nodded and walked away.

Lulu noticed Chet Harris gazing into the travel agency window. As soon as he was gone, Sally came out of the travel agency, and Lulu continued following her, with her film rolling. She noticed that Sally's big purse wasn't flat anymore. It bulged quite a bit.

When Sally got home, she turned on the lights in the living room. The window shades were up, so Lulu could see in. The room looked awfully drab, with peeling paint. And there was only a small couch and a couple of faded rugs.

Wow, Sally's awfully poor, Lulu decided as she followed her movements with her Minicam. *So how can she afford to go to Bora Bora?* Sally went into the bedroom, where the shades were down.

"I guess that's all for today," Lulu said under her breath. She turned off her camera and headed home.

When Lulu opened the apartment door, the phone was ringing. "Lulu, where were you?" asked Toby. "You forgot to come to Rachel's basketball tryout!"

"Oh, gosh, I did." Lulu felt horrible. "Did she make the team?"

"Yes," said Toby dryly. "But that's not the point. Rachel was so upset that you weren't there. Remember, you promised to film her face when she made the team?"

Lulu groaned. "I'll call Rachel right away and tell her I'm sorry."

Toby's voice grew soft. "Lulu, are you sure you still want to be in the Angel Club?"

"Of course I do!" Lulu said. "What a silly question."

As soon as she hung up, the phone rang again. It was Val.

"I know why you called," Lulu blurted. "Toby just told me about the basketball tryouts. I'll phone Rachel to apologize right—"

"That's not why I called." Val's voice sounded frightened. "Someone stole five thousand dollars from my mom's travel agency today."

"You're kidding! When? What time?"

"Right after school. Mom went to the bathroom, and when she came back the money was gone."

"Val!" Lulu lowered her voice. "Sally Jillian was there this afternoon. I have a tape of her going into the store with a thin purse and coming out with a fat one! I bet she took the money!"

Val's voice rose. "Sally would never do a thing like that. How can you suspect her of such a thing?"

"How else can she afford a trip to Bora Bora?" Lulu persisted. "You should see her house. There's nothing in it!"

Val's voice grew angrier than Lulu had ever heard it. "Lulu, I have to tell you something. You are turning into a mean, suspicious person, and I don't like it! What's happened to you?"

Val didn't wait for Lulu to answer. "I don't want to talk anymore tonight. I'm hanging up right now!"

Lulu held the phone dumbly as the dial tone buzzed at her. *How am I acting different?* she asked herself, and decided that she wasn't.

But she instantly forgot to call Rachel.

9

A Broken Friendship Bracelet

Lulu shivered a little as she sat in her room alone. "Val is changing, not me," she said out loud. "I wish she'd grow up." Lulu decided to take a nice, warm, comforting bubble bath.

After she filled the tub with pink bubbles, Lulu lay back, pretending to be a famous director relaxing in her Hollywood mansion.

Plink! A silver-wrapped chocolate kiss splashed into the tub.

Lulu giggled. "Is that you, Celeste?"

"Have a hug, too," Celeste whispered. Another chocolate fell into Lulu's outstretched palm.

"I know you haven't called," Celeste said

quickly. "This is just a social visit!" She curtsied in midair. "I hope you don't mind."

"It's fine. I was feeling a little lonely," she admitted. She popped the chocolate into her mouth.

Celeste settled herself comfortably on a little hill of foam. "I wanted to talk to you about movies. I've been watching so many, and I wish there was a way I could become an actress. Everybody admires them so much. And they get to have their names up in lights."

"That's right." Lulu nodded, unwrapping the other chocolate. "Directors get lots of attention, too."

Celeste let a chocolate melt in her mouth. "Let's play a game to see if I'm a good actress. I'll imitate a famous actor or actress for you, and you see if you can guess who it is."

"Okay." Lulu settled back in the tub as Celeste took a deep breath and launched into a chorus of "Over the Rainbow."

"Judy Garland," said Lulu promptly. "But you don't sound like her at all."

"How about this?" Celeste made her face look sort of blank. "Mama always told me, 'Stupid is as stupid does.' "

"That's Forrest Gump!" Lulu giggled. "But you don't sound like Tom Hanks."

"I guess I need more practice." Celeste sighed. "I'll go watch some more movies. Ta-ta! Call me if you need me!" As she flew off, Celeste waved her arm and created an enormous hill of rose-scented golden bubbles.

"Thank you!" Lulu lay back in the luxurious bubbles. "Celeste is so great," she crooned. "It's a shame I don't have any problems for her to solve."

Feeling calm and confident after her bath, Lulu did all of her homework. "Boy, is Ms. Fisher going to faint when she finds out I'm prepared again."

The next day, Lulu tried calling Rachel to apologize for missing her tryout, but no one answered the Summers' phone. Lulu tried Val's number. She wanted to talk to Val and convince her that she was just fine and that Val was overreacting. But Val's mother answered and said that Val was busy helping her younger stepsister with a class project and that she would call Lulu back later.

Finally, after what seemed like hours, the telephone rang and Lulu ran to answer it. "Val, let's have a soda together, okay? I want to talk about our conversation last night."

"Sure, okay." Val sounded just a little hopeful.

They met at the Angel Clock and headed up Main Street. "Val," Lulu began, "I think you're totally wrong about me. I haven't changed at all. I'm just using my movie skills to keep my dad from ruining his life—and mine."

"Oh, really?" Val stopped walking.

"Right. And I'm planning to sneak into Sally's house and see if I can find the money she took. Why don't you come with me?"

"Lulu!" Val looked horrified. "Are you out of your mind? Don't you dare go snooping in Sally's house! How would you like it if someone did that to you?"

Lulu looked puzzled. "But I'm doing it for you, Val. Don't you want to find your mother's money?"

"I'll tell you what I want!" Val yelled. "I don't want to talk to you anymore. Not ever. You've turned into a horrible person."

Val ripped off her friendship bracelet and tossed it at Lulu's feet. Then she burst into tears and ran off.

Lulu stood there in shock. *How can Val be so ungrateful?* she asked herself. She sadly picked up the bracelet and stuck it into her pocket.

Walking alone, Lulu tried to forget about what Val had said.

When she passed Derek's store, he called out to her. "Lulu, I see you have your Minicam. Why don't you take a shot of the store? For historical purposes?"

"Sure," Lulu agreed, and took a quick shot of him standing in front.

Then Sheriff Perkins appeared. "Hey, Sheriff!"

Derek said. "Come and film Lulu buying a book."

"Okeydoke."

After he shot the two of them together, Sheriff Perkins said, "Have you looked at the film I took of you the other day, Lulu?"

"Um, no." Lulu shook her head.

"Ah, well," he sighed, and left. Lulu walked toward Sally's house, but on the way, she took a few more shots of the railway station. It was almost finished. The building was shiny red, mostly, with just one section left to be cleaned.

"Hey, Mr. Harris," Lulu called. "I still have to interview you!"

"Not now," he said grumpily. "I'm busy. I wish you'd stop pestering me."

Lulu left reluctantly, but then, on Main Street, she caught sight of Sally.

The accountant was wearing a blue silk dress and high heels. Lulu hid behind the corner of a building and watched Sally talking to a meter maid and petting a scruffy little dog.

Lulu heard Sally say, "Doesn't anyone own him?"

"No." The meter maid shook her head. "I don't see a collar or ID."

"Poor guy." Sally squatted down and put out her hand. The dog sniffed gingerly, and then licked it. "Good boy," Sally crooned, and petted him gently on the head. Then she said, "Would you like to come home with me?"

The dog wagged his tail. "Come on, then," Sally said, smiling. "I've got a yard; you'll like it at my house. All you need is a bath, some food, and some loving."

As Lulu followed Sally, the phrase from *Forrest Gump* kept running through her head. "Stupid is as stupid does." It wasn't Celeste's voice or Val's. It was her own.

Lulu saw Sally stop in the convenience store and buy some dog food. When she reached her house, she fed the dog in the kitchen. He wolfed down the whole can, he was so hungry. And Lulu could see it wasn't the cheap brand, either.

If only Sally goes out again, I can climb into her window and begin my search, Lulu thought.

But Sally didn't go anywhere. She fixed a tunafish salad sandwich and sat at the kitchen table. While she nibbled at her dinner, she read a book. Every now and then Sally gazed up, as if she were looking for something or someone. Lulu almost felt sorry for her. She knew how much *she* hated to eat alone. *Ooops! I'd better get home for my own dinner.*

Lulu raced home to supper with her dad. "What'll it be, mademoiselle?" he asked. "The usual caviar and cornflakes?"

Lulu smiled. "Sure."

70

"Or shall we have tuna-noodle casserole for a change?"

Tuna? thought Lulu. *Sally's eating tuna, too.* "The casserole," Lulu said, playing along. She tried not to think about the connection. The food was delicious, and there was chocolate pudding for dessert.

"Is mademoiselle pleased?" her dad asked when dinner was over.

"Très bien!" Lulu smiled. Everything felt normal again. "I'll take care of the dishes," she offered. "You sit down and take it easy. I know your feet hurt from standing up all day."

"Well, aren't you an angel?" Mr. Bliss said. He went into the living room. "I guess I'll play some solitaire."

While Lulu washed the dishes, she could hear her dad shuffling the cards. He seemed to lose a lot of games. He sighed a lot, dealing the cards again and again.

Lulu glanced into the room once, and noticed that her dad's face looked sad and wistful. She felt a little stab of pity. He looked lonely, but how could he be when he had her?

Her dad's expression reminded Lulu of a look she'd seen on someone else's face recently. In a moment, she realized whose it was: Sally Jillian's, just an hour ago, as she was eating her dinner.

Lulu gulped and tried to put both faces out of her

mind. She was grateful when the phone rang, and it was Toby.

"Derek just got zillions of books delivered. He can hardly walk around in his store. So the Angel Club has volunteered to go there first thing tomorrow and help. It's Sunday, so everyone can do it. Can you come?"

"Sure!" Lulu agreed. "I'll be there with bells on!"

"Forget the bells," said Toby. "It's noisy enough with Derek's cockatoo around."

"Right." Lulu hung up and did her homework. Math wasn't so hard if you kept up with it every day. It was boring, but it wasn't hard.

When she closed her eyes to go to sleep, Lulu felt restless. "Celeste," she called out quietly. "Can you help me fall asleep?"

Instantly Celeste appeared over her bed in a blur of green ruffles and pink light. "You called me! I'm really thrilled, Lulu. But you know, I could do more for you than just help you sleep. I could help you—"

"Celeste, everything's fine, really," said Lulu, protesting a little too much.

"All right." Celeste sighed and began singing softly. She sang a lullaby that Lulu's mother used to sing to her as a baby, though Lulu did not remember it. As the music played, Lulu's room filled with gently blinking silver stars.

"Make a wish," Celeste told Lulu.

Lulu's Mixed-Up Movie

"I want my movie to come out! I want it to be the most fascinating movie ever made in Angel Corners." Lulu hugged her pillow and fell asleep.

"Now, which movie did she mean?" Celeste wondered as she flew back to the Angel Academy.

10

Bad News! Bad News!

The next day, Lulu ate breakfast while her father went jogging.

She put on her denim overalls and her *Beauty and the Beast* T-shirt and left to take a walk, loaded down with her Minicam and plenty of film.

As she rushed down the street, she almost ran right into Mayor Witty. "Good morning, Lulu. Don't you look chipper? I'm feeling fine myself! The work on the railroad station is ahead of schedule. It should be finished soon."

"Really? I'd better go shoot more film."

Lulu hardly recognized the building, it was so

changed. She taped it again from all different angles and, since the workmen had the day off, interviewed the stationmaster.

He talked for a long time about how many hundreds of new tourists would be coming. Finally, he looked at his watch and said, "I have to go home now. It's almost noon."

"Almost noon? The time went by so fast!" Lulu gasped. "I was supposed to meet the Angel Club hours ago."

Lulu rushed to Derek's bookstore, but the lights were out and the door was closed. BACK IN HALF AN HOUR, said a sign on the door.

Lulu gazed down the street and saw Derek and her friends walking toward the Sweet Shop. She pulled out her camera to get a shot of them, hoping it would show that she really did care, even though she was late, and filmed them as they went in—and Chet Harris with his mismatched socks came out. She quickly put her camera away, knowing how annoyed he was getting with her, and followed her friends into the store.

"Where have you been?" Toby asked. "We've unpacked and shelved boxes and boxes of books!" Toby and Rachel looked dusty, disheveled, and irritated.

"I'm sorry," Lulu said. "I really am."

Val wouldn't look at Lulu at all. She sat in the booth, gazing down.

"We're taking a break," Rachel explained. "Derek's treating us to ice-cream sodas."

"Lulu, you have one, too," Derek insisted. "I'll be putting you to work as soon as we get back."

"Derek, you're a peach." Lulu smiled at him.

When they finished their sodas, Derek said teasingly, "Come on, girls, it's back to the salt mines."

When they reached his store, he said, "Hmm, that's funny. I don't remember leaving the door open." He hurried inside, and the girls followed him.

Derek opened the cash register. His eyes grew wide. "All the money is gone! I took four hundred dollars out of the bank yesterday. Where is it?"

"It must be there," Toby said confidently. "Mom and Dad put big bills under the drawer at the bakery. You probably forgot that you stuck them there."

Derek lifted the drawer, and saw nothing.

Lulu spoke up. "Derek, I passed the store just after you and the Angel Club left, and the door was closed. That means the robbery must have happened just a few minutes ago. Maybe the person is still nearby!"

Everybody rushed out the door.

Lulu turned on her Minicam to capture the

scene. All she got was Toby's mom carrying some laundry. Then Zeb Burgess hurried by with a few new video games, but that was all.

No, it wasn't! Lulu pointed her camera a little farther down the block and focused to adjust for the distance. There was Sally Jillian in a running suit jogging toward her home with her scruffy dog—and carrying a bulky canvas bag. *Aha!* thought Lulu. *Gotcha!*

Lulu turned off her camera.

"Bad news! Bad news!" shrieked Ezra the cockatoo.

"Ezra, shut up!" Toby scolded. "Derek, what are you going to do?"

"I don't know," he said, shaking his head. "This is a heck of a way to begin a new business. I was going to use that money to buy a big sign. I was hoping it would attract tourists."

"I just saw Sally Jillian running away with a big sack of something!" Lulu said quickly. "Maybe she did it. If we went after her, we could catch her with the goods and I could get it on film."

The Angel Club and Derek looked at Lulu as if she had lost her mind.

"Lulu!" cried Val. "Get serious and get Sally Jillian out of your mean little mind."

Derek was gentler. He said, "Sally always passes by here when she's out jogging. She's a friend of mine. She even helped me sort out my finances so I could afford to buy this store. She would never steal from me." Derek's voice grew softer. "You girls go on home. I could use some time alone."

"Sure, Derek, sure," they all said, and Toby patted his shoulder as they left.

Outside, she turned on Lulu. "Sally Jillian was out running with your father this morning. They stopped at our bakery and Sally bought some rolls. That's what was in her bag."

Lulu shrugged. Maybe Sally wasn't the one who robbed the travel agency and the bookstore. But if *she* wasn't, who was? After all, Lulu had Sally on tape at both scenes of the crimes.

"C'mon, Toby," said Rachel, "it's time for basketball practice." They walked off together.

Val was about to say something to Lulu, but instead just shook her head and ran off toward Hickory Hill.

Lulu stood on the corner, feeling more alone than she had ever felt in her life.

11

Angelic Workouts

Celeste hovered nearby, hoping Lulu would call for her, but she didn't. Feeling restless, and a little lonely, too, she flew back to the Angel Academy.

Celeste found all her friends doing Angelic Exercises.

"Now, angels," Florinda was saying, "the work we do requires incredible stamina. We can't possibly do it well unless we are in tip-top condition."

"Tip-top!" echoed Merrie, turning cartwheels faster than the speed of light.

Serena was wearing a pretty spangled pink leotard. She did the splits the way Toby had taught her.

Amber, dressed in an amber workout suit, was

jogging around in a neat circle, over and over.

"Here's Celeste," Amber said, happy for an excuse to stop and catch her breath.

"Let's all take a break," Florinda suggested. She poured the angels tall glasses of heavenly juices.

"Lulu is totally ignoring me," Celeste reported. "It's so frustrating! But I've been busy watching movies while keeping my eye on her. I've done a lot of research on snacks at the candy counter, too. I've brought you all some goodies."

Celeste reached into one of her dress ruffles and retrieved four bags of candy. "Here are Smarties for you, Amber."

"Thank you. Will they make me smarter?" Amber asked.

"Try them and see," Celeste teased. "But I think you're incredibly smart already. And I brought Life Savers for you, Serena, since you practically saved Toby's life."

"Thank you!" Serena smiled gratefully. "I was so busy concentrating on cakes at Toby's bakery that I didn't have time to explore the candy situation."

"And I have Butterfingers for you, Merrie," Celeste said, laughing.

Merrie giggled. "Because I drop things and keep landing upside down?"

"Oh *no*," Celeste answered, but she giggled, too. "And I have Starbursts for you, Florinda."

"That's very sweet of you," Florinda said. "Of course, as soon as we finish these treats, we'll need to work out extra hard."

"What has been happening at the Angel Academy while I've been gone?" Celeste asked.

"Well," began Merrie, "there's going to be an Angel of the Month contest. I'm entering."

"So am I!" said Serena.

"Me, too," Amber sang.

"I'll be sorry to miss it," Celeste said regretfully. "But I have my hands full with Lulu."

"Before you go," Merrie said, "let's do some gymnastics together."

"All right," Celeste agreed. "Let's do some quick cartwheels. We'll pretend that we're Angel Corners cheerleaders."

Serena and Merrie did a few small cartwheels. Their dresses hardly fluttered.

"Come on, angels! You can do better than that!" Florinda urged.

Amber did a bigger cartwheel all around the Big Dipper.

"That's much better!" Florinda praised her.

"Now, watch this!" Celeste smiled. She spread her wings, took a deep breath—and cartwheeled over the Milky Way.

"A+!" Florinda shouted.

"Hooray for me!" Celeste beamed brightly. Then

she happily somersaulted all the way back to Lulu.

Celeste arrived at Lulu's house to find her sleeping, but she could see her dreams weren't very peaceful. "You have so much spirit!" Celeste murmured. "But everyone needs an angel sometimes. I wish you'd realize that."

12

Arrested!

The next morning, as Lulu left for school, she noticed that one of the films her dad had picked for the store that day was *Romeo and Juliet*.

"Tonight we have to have a talk," Mr. Bliss told Lulu. "I've been putting it off, but I can't anymore."

Lulu swallowed hard. She got through school that day with some difficulty. Val was home sick. Lulu wanted to call her but was still too angry. Val had been horrible, yelling and throwing her bracelet.

After school, Lulu dropped in at Derek's store to see if anyone had found his money.

"No." He shook his head. "I reported the theft to Sheriff Perkins. He's making patrols more often from now on. He says everyone in town is edgy.

We've had two robberies in a row. They still don't know who stole the money from Val's mother."

Lulu left and took a few final shots of the railway station. Again, she couldn't interview Chet. He was up on the roof, out of shouting distance.

Lulu went over to Sally's house and saw her out in the yard with her new dog. He already looked much healthier, running around and fetching a stick.

Hiding behind a thick catalpa tree, Lulu turned on her camera.

Sally was gazing up at an airplane overhead. "Oh, Romeo!" she crooned. "Just imagine, this time next week, we'll be in Bora Bora!"

Romeo! Bora Bora! And Daddy was watching Romeo and Juliet *this morning!* Lulu clicked off the camera. *They are running away! This is the proof!*

Lulu blinked back tears as she turned to leave. Suddenly, she caught the scent of Old Spice. Sheriff Perkins was standing right behind her. "Young lady," he said, "you are under arrest."

"What? Me?" Lulu gulped.

"Yes, you, Lulu. I have warned you about stalking people with your camera. I was checking Sally's house because she told me she's been frightened. She was afraid because she kept sensing that somebody was watching her."

"What's going on?" Sally called out nervously, hearing them.

"Everything's fine. It's Sheriff Perkins," he answered. "I found your stalker, Sally." He took Lulu's hand. "Come on. I'm taking you down to the station."

As they got into the sheriff's car, Lulu could see the sad, pained look on Sally's face.

I can't believe this is happening, Lulu told herself, trying not to burst into tears. "Celeste!" she whispered, "I need you."

"Here I am!" Celeste appeared on the seat beside her. "I'll stay with you, I promise."

When they reached the station, Sheriff Perkins phoned Lulu's father. While he did, Celeste sat next to Lulu, stroking her hair. "There, there," she kept repeating, and Lulu calmed down a little.

"Do you want to tell me what's going on, Lulu?" whispered Celeste.

"I guess I better wait until my dad gets here and explain it to him. Thanks anyway," said Lulu. Honestly, she didn't know *what* to say or where to begin.

She heard the sheriff explain the situation to her dad and hang up. "He'll be here in five minutes," Sheriff Perkins told her.

"I didn't know I was scaring Sally," Lulu blurted out. "I'm sorry. I really am."

"I'm sure you are. And so am I." The sheriff looked as unhappy as Lulu.

Celeste wanted to make the whole situation disappear. But she knew she must not interfere. This was one of those problems Lulu must solve herself.

When Mr. Bliss arrived, he had a private talk with the sheriff. "All right," Lulu heard Sheriff Perkins say. "I'm releasing her to your custody."

Mr. Bliss took Lulu's hand. "Let's go. We'll talk when we get home."

The silence was awful as they drove away. Celeste sat in the backseat where Lulu could see her in the rearview mirror. When they reached the apartment, Mr. Bliss sat Lulu down at the kitchen table. "I need a strong cup of coffee for this," he said, and put on a pot to percolate.

"This is something I *can* do," Celeste decided. She made the water boil faster, and the coffee was done in a minute.

"Hmm, that was fast." Mr. Bliss stared at the pot, then gratefully poured himself a cup.

"Um, Dad—" Lulu began.

"I'll do the talking," her father said sternly. He sat down and faced Lulu. "What you did to Sally was terrible! Do you know how scared she was? Young lady, you are grounded for two weeks. Furthermore, you cannot use your camera for quite a while."

Lulu groaned. So did Celeste.

"But I have a lot more to say," Mr. Bliss continued, his face suddenly flushing bright red. "First, I want to tell you that I have been going out with Sally Jillian."

Lulu nodded. It was almost a relief to hear the truth straight out.

"I should have told you about it long ago. But I didn't, and do you want to know why?"

Lulu shrugged.

Her dad's voice grew husky. "Because I was afraid of hurting your feelings. I could tell that you didn't want our life to change one bit. And that made me feel really guilty about going out with someone."

"Dad—I—" Lulu blurted.

"I'm not finished yet." Mr. Bliss leaned forward and took one of Lulu's hands. "You know I love you very much, but I have my own life to lead, too. I have every right to a life of my own, just as you have to a life of your own. It's time you begin to realize that."

Lulu nodded. She remembered the sad look she had seen on her dad's face. She wanted him to be happy—she really did.

Mr. Bliss squeezed Lulu's hand. "Seeing Sally doesn't mean I love you any less, you know. I could never do that."

"Oh, Daddy!" Lulu's eyes filled with tears. "But Sally is the thief! I have her on film going into the travel agency with an empty bag and coming out with a full one! And I saw her right after Derek's store was robbed! She's so poor, how else could she afford tickets to Bora Bora?"

"Come here, sweetie."

Lulu rushed over to her dad, who reached out and caught her in a hug. "You have to be very careful about jumping to conclusions, Lulu. You've made some serious mistakes. Sally is not a criminal! Just because you saw her at the travel agency and the bookstore doesn't mean she is guilty. She went to the travel agency to get brochures on Bora Bora resorts, and she and I had been jogging and shopping before you saw her at Derek's. I also know that she won those tickets to Bora Bora by entering a contest in an accounting magazine."

"And you're going with her and leaving me behind!" cried Lulu.

Mr. Bliss looked perplexed. *"What?"*

"Aren't you going to Bora Bora with Sally?"

"What gave you that idea? *She's* going, with a girlfriend."

"Then who is Romeo?" Lulu asked.

"Romeo? Besides being a character from a Shakespeare play? Romeo is Sally's dog." Lulu's father tweaked her nose.

"Oh, Daddy, I was so worried!" Lulu cried for a while, and her father stroked her head.

"You're my Lulu," he crooned. "You'll always be my Lulu."

"I acted so horribly," Lulu admitted. "I'm really sorry." When she finished crying, a soft pink hankie appeared in her hand, thanks to Celeste. Lulu blew her nose, then asked, "But what about all those South Seas movies you were watching, and the book you ordered from Derek's store? If you're not going to Bora Bora—"

Her dad smiled. "Because I was planning a surprise for your birthday—a snorkeling trip for us."

"Oh, boy!" Lulu shook her head. "Have *I* been confused."

"You can say that again," Mr. Bliss said. "Are we all straightened out now? I have my life, of which you are the leading, but not the only, star. You have your life, which I cherish and guide the best I can—but it is yours. And if you are going to grow up to be a director, you're going to have to start viewing life with your own two eyes before you put it willy-nilly on film."

As fatherly speeches go, it was a pretty good one. It could have been a lot worse!

"Let's skip caviar and cornflakes, mademoiselle, and go out for dinner tonight," suggested Mr. Bliss.

"Tell him you'll cook," Celeste whispered. "I'll help you."

"I'd rather stay home and cook," Lulu said. "You sit down and rest." Within twenty minutes Lulu and Celeste had prepared ginger chicken and rice, shrimp toast, and brownies.

As they ate, Lulu asked quietly, "Do you think Sally or Sheriff Perkins will hate me forever?"

"I don't think so."

"I'll write them apologies," Lulu decided. "Sally is a nice person, I know. I was just trying to convince myself that she wasn't."

"I do think you'll like her, when you give her a chance."

"I'll try," Lulu promised.

"Hey," Lulu's dad said, "why don't you show me your film of the railroad station? I haven't forgotten my promise to help you with the editing."

"But it's on the same tape as my shots of Sally," Lulu said, embarrassed.

"We can edit those out."

Lulu put the videotape in the VCR, rewinding it to the beginning. They watched the railway station before the sandblasting and the workmen eating breakfast. "Good zoom," praised Lulu's dad, seeing Chet Harris and his mismatched socks.

Then there were shots of Rachel and Toby practicing basketball and Val cheering. Lulu smiled as she saw the Angel Club. Then she swallowed hard.

Lately, she had hardly seen her friends at all.

There was more film of sandblasting, followed by the shot of Lulu lurking in the doorway. That was the shot the sheriff had insisted on taking when Lulu had followed Sally to the travel agency. Lulu stopped the film.

"I look so angry!" she whispered. She suddenly understood why Sheriff Perkins had insisted on taking her picture: he wanted Lulu to see for herself how weirdly she was acting. And, boy, did it show!

Her dad groaned as he saw Sally leaving the travel agency. Then Lulu saw herself again, with Derek, in the bookstore. "I look so sad!" she moaned.

"And mad, too," added her father. Lulu suddenly remembered what she had told Rachel when she had seen the tape of herself playing basketball: "Sometimes it helps to see yourself from the outside."

I'm seeing myself, all right, and I don't like what I'm seeing. She began thinking about her friends, and how she had been treating them lately. *I let Val down when she wanted my help, and I was really nasty to her, too.*

Lulu thought about how disappointed Rachel had been when Lulu forgot to come to her tryouts. And she thought about Toby and how angry she was when Lulu forgot to help them at Derek's store. Toby had even asked Lulu if she still wanted to be in the Angel Club.

I do! Lulu told herself. Now the film showed Zeb Burgess walking down the street. "Boy! What Val wouldn't give for that picture!" Lulu said with a laugh.

And that's when she got her great idea. "Dad, I need to do a lot of editing and copying tonight. Will you help me?"

"Sure," he said. And then Lulu explained her plan.

That night, Lulu told Celeste, "I should have called you so much sooner. My friends were right. I do need an angel, just like everyone else."

Celeste glittered thankfully. "Oh, I'm so glad you want me!"

"I want you forever!" Lulu hugged Celeste close.

13

Mini-Movies

The next morning in school, Lulu wrote notes to Val, Rachel, and Lulu: *Please come to an emergency meeting of the Angel Club at lunchtime. This is urgent!*

When the lunch bell rang, everyone gathered in the cafeteria. Val was wearing a new violet blouse. It made her eyes, already glowing with curiosity, incredibly vivid.

"Oh, Val, I've missed you so much!" Lulu said. "And I'm so sorry!"

Val broke into a smile. "Lulu!" She reached out and they hugged. "What's been going on? You have to tell me everything."

Rachel beamed at them. "Lulu, you look happier than you've been in ages."

"I *am* happier." Lulu smiled at Rachel, who was now wearing an Angel Corners basketball-team shirt that matched Toby's.

"Did you call the meeting to tell us you're happy?" Toby asked. "That's okay with me."

"No!" Lulu smiled. "I called the meeting to apologize for the way I've been acting lately. I've been feeling totally sorry for myself and angry at everyone else. I've let you all down, I know it."

Rachel, Toby, and Val nodded.

"But I promise to make it up to you, and to the Angel Club.

"You'll never believe this, but last night Sheriff Perkins arrested me for stalking Sally! Thank goodness Celeste was there in a flash. She sat with me in the squad car and at the station until Dad came. I've never been so embarrassed or frightened."

The Angel Club expressed their amazement and support. Val put her arm around her friend, but all she could say was, "Oh, Lulu . . ."

Lulu laughed. "I'll get over it. Anyway, last night, Dad and I had a good talk. He told me that he *is* seeing Sally. I think, after a while, I'll get used to it. I want Dad to be happy. I've been selfish about him. And you were all right about my jumping to conclusions about her. Boy, have I learned my lesson!"

"I'm so glad things are better." Val squeezed Lulu's hand.

"How did your railway station movie come out?" Rachel asked.

"I was just coming to that. Dad helped me splice the tape together so that it flows really well. But there were a lot of other scenes on my tape, too. We came up with a good name for it: *Lulu's Mixed-Up Movie*. And that's where all of you come in."

Lulu reached into her backpack and took out three gift-wrapped packages. "Here, Val, you open yours first."

"It's a tape." Val read the title: *Val's Movie*.

"I'll tell you what's on it," Lulu said eagerly. "A shot of Zeb Burgess looking so cute as he walks along Main Street. You can play it on your VCR and kiss him sweet dreams every night."

Val blushed. "I will!"

Rachel opened her package. "I have a tape called *Rachel's Movie*."

"It's the footage of you and Toby practicing basketball." Rachel smiled at her. "I thought you'd want it to show your mother and to keep reminding yourself what a good player you are."

"Oh, I do," Rachel gushed. "Thanks."

"I wonder what's in my box," Toby teased. "Right—a tape!" She read the title: *Toby's Movie*.

"It's the same tape as Rachel's. You're doing such a good job coaching her that maybe you could use the tape to help you get a basketball scholarship someday."

"Whew!" Toby grinned. "You sure think ahead."

As the Angel Club ate lunch together, Lulu asked everyone to tell her what they'd been doing.

"Well," said Toby, "I've been helping Derek some more. Poor guy. Now he can't afford a sign for his store."

"My mom wishes the sheriff could find out who took her money, too."

"Hmm, we still have two unsolved mysteries," Lulu said.

But they didn't stay unsolved for long.

14

Help! Celeste! Help!

After school, Lulu wrote a letter to Sally. She worked on it a long time.

Dear Sally,
    I am so sorry! I didn't mean to scare you. I know I have no excuse for what I did. I was pretty mixed-up. I feel so guilty.
    I am really sorry. I hope you can come over and have dinner sometime. I am a great cook, and my father isn't too bad, either.
                    With all my apologies,
                    Lulu Bliss

Lulu felt a lot better after she wrote the note. She

couldn't quite face Sally yet, so she mailed it, with a cheerful Marx Brothers stamp on the envelope.

Next she went and apologized to Sheriff Perkins. "I know you took that movie of me so I could see from the outside how I was really acting," Lulu said. "That was very clever of you."

"Oh." He flushed. "Sometimes I get a good idea or two."

Lulu left his office and went to take some final shots of the railroad station. By the time she was finished, it was beginning to get dark.

As Lulu headed home, she passed Frank's Fabulous Clothing store. Frank DeCarlo was out front, pacing around. "I'm waiting for the sheriff," he said. "Someone ran into my shop a few minutes ago, tried on the suit in the window, and then grabbed all my money and left." Mr. DeCarlo laughed. "He should've taken a pair of socks, too! The ones he had on didn't even match!" He put his head in his hands.

A light went on in Lulu's head. His socks didn't match? Who else besides Sally had been near Val's mom's agency *and* Derek's bookstore when the crimes were committed! Chet Harris!

"Celeste," Lulu whispered, but was cut short by a voice shrieking, *"Hurry! Hurry! The train is leaving! Hurry!"*

"Okay! Celeste! I hear you!" Lulu set off for the station.

But when she'd gone just a few steps, Hortense Heft appeared from out of nowhere.

"Hi, Lulu," she said. "I'm just back from my round-the-world honeymoon. I have so much to tell you about the horseback riding in Italy."

"Um, could you tell me another time?" Lulu begged, and, not waiting for an answer, rushed away.

But after a few more steps, Lulu ran smack into Mrs. McWithers, Felicia's mother.

"Well, I never!" she sputtered. "Look what you've done. My hat fell off and it's ruined!"

"I'm sorry!" Lulu said, trying to pull away. Finally, she succeeded and dashed off.

When she reached the railway station, nobody was there, and it was very dark. No, somebody *was* there: Lulu saw Chet Harris, carrying a suitcase. She ran up to him.

"Hey, stop!" Lulu yelled. "Now I know why you wouldn't finish the interview without your mask! You're the thief! You can't run away with all that money and Mr. DeCarlo's suit!"

"Listen, you," Chet Harris exploded. "I'm sick of your snooping! And now I'm going to have to shut you up for good!" The tall, burly man took a step toward Lulu.

"Help! Celeste, help me!" Lulu shouted.

Suddenly the train appeared, coming down the

track. The light on the front of the engine grew brighter and brighter. The thief tried to shield his eyes as he stumbled toward Lulu. "Ouch!" he yelled as he tripped over some sandblasting equipment, falling down with a thud. He fell hard, and was out cold!

"Oh, gosh!" Lulu gasped for breath.

She was shielding her own eyes from the bright light when the train shimmered brightly—and disappeared. Celeste appeared in its place, glowing and smiling, her ruffles all aflutter. "Wasn't I bright?" she said, beaming.

"You turned yourself into—a train!" Lulu was astounded. "You are definitely the brightest creature in the world." She rushed over and hugged Celeste. "You saved my life."

Celeste hugged her back happily. "It probably won't be the last time I do."

After a moment, Celeste said, "Look, Lulu." Chet Harris's suitcase was open, and inside were piles of money.

Lulu grinned. "Derek is going to get his money back, and so are Val's mom and Mr. DeCarlo."

Lulu dialed 911 so the sheriff could come and get the thief. While she and Celeste waited, Lulu began thinking things over. "Hey, Celeste," she said, "if you didn't want me to get into trouble, why did you yell at me to run to the railway station?"

"That wasn't me!" Celeste said, horrified. "That was Derek's cockatoo."

"Oh!" Lulu giggled.

"And I did try to stop you from going there. If I had told you directly not to go, you probably wouldn't have listened. So I impersonated Hortense Heft and Mrs. McWithers. Each time, I tried to delay you, but you kept running away."

Lulu's eyes went wide. "You were them—I mean, they were you, too? Celeste, you deserve an Academy Award." Lulu laughed until tears came to her eyes.

"I think so, too." Celeste beamed.

The sound of sirens began filling the air, and Sheriff Perkins arrived. "You again!" he said to Lulu. But he cheered up considerably when he saw that Lulu had caught the thief.

It was a little difficult telling the sheriff the story of how she had single-handedly captured the thief, but how could she explain that her guardian angel had turned into a train, blinding him?

"After Mr. DeCarlo mentioned the thief's mismatched socks—see, I wear mismatched socks, too"—she pulled up her pant legs to reveal one red and one purple sock—"I remembered that Chet Harris did, too. We directors have to pay attention to that kind of detail."

The sheriff sighed. "Please stick to the story, Miss Bliss."

"Yes, sir," said Lulu, buying time to figure out how to tell the rest of the story without mentioning Celeste. "I thought, *Where else would he go but the train station to wait for the next train out of town?* Well, when I showed up, he came after me, but he didn't look where he was going and tripped and fell. He knocked himself out."

"You could have wound up hurt pretty bad, young lady," said the sheriff. "But it sounds like you have a guardian angel watching over you. I have to get this thug into jail or I'd give you a ride home. You'll be all right—and go straight home?"

"Yes, sir," said Lulu.

"And let's try and stay out of each other's way for a while—deal?" asked the sheriff, smiling.

"Deal." They shook hands on it.

After Sheriff Perkins drove off with Chet Harris handcuffed in the backseat, Celeste asked Lulu, "Can you stay out of danger for a few hours? Florinda is summoning me back to the Angel Academy."

"Sure." Lulu smiled at her. "At least I'll try!"

So Celeste flew back to Florinda.

15

Up in Lights

When Celeste reached the Crystal Classroom, it was dark, and nobody was there. A sign on the door said:

ALL CLASSES ARE MEETING TODAY IN THE STAR-SAPPHIRE WORKOUT CENTER. PLEASE FLY THERE AT ALL POSSIBLE SPEED!

"That's odd," Celeste said. She nibbled nervously on some Skittles and headed toward the Workout Center. It was a zillion miles away, on the other side of the campus. Just flying there was a workout.

As Celeste neared the entrance, she noticed it

was awfully quiet. Usually, there were clusters of angels hovering around.

The lights were out, too. How odd.

Celeste opened the door and flew inside.

"Surprise!" came a chorus of angelic voices, and then the diamond-and-emerald lights glittered on!

One hundred angels had formed a huge pyramid, and they all began cheering:

THE ANGEL OF THE MONTH,
SHE IS THE BEST,
SHE'S OUR VERY OWN,
ANGEL CELESTE!

"Me? I'm the Angel of the Month?" Celeste lit up all of heaven, she was so happy.

"Yes," said Florinda, flying over to Celeste. She enveloped her warmly, and another huge cheer filled the heavens:

CELESTE IS GREAT
WHEN IT'S SUNNY OR RAINING!
SHE IS THE BRIGHTEST
ANGEL-IN-TRAINING!

"Oh, gosh!" Celeste flushed, but she loved the attention.

Florinda announced to all the assembled angels, "Celeste did an absolutely splendid job on her first visit to earth."

"She saved Lulu's life!" Amber said in awe. She gave Celeste a hug. "I'm really sorry that I said you weren't the right angel for her."

"That's all right," Celeste responded generously.

"And you had so much fun in Angel Corners," added Serena. "It took me so much longer to realize that earth is a really welcoming place for angels."

Merrie beamed, too. "I only turned into a bird, but you turned into a train! Let's do some stuff together sometimes. Imagine the chaos we can create in Angel Corners!"

"I can imagine!" Florinda said, rolling her eyes. Then her face turned serious. "Celeste, here is a token of our appreciation for all your good work." She handed Celeste a glittery golden box.

"Oooh," Celeste said, and gasped when she opened it. Inside was a ring with a huge diamond star, and in all the facets of the diamond were images of Lulu.

"That's my girl!" Celeste said proudly. "I'll wear this ring for all eternity."

Celeste's party went on for quite a while. There was tribute after tribute and toast after toast to her intelligence, joyfulness, and imagination.

When it was over, Celeste suddenly heard Lulu calling for help. She beamed. "Lulu wants me! Oh, it feels so wonderful to be wanted."

She flew away from the party and hurried to Lulu's side. Lulu was hugging her pillow, looking pensive.

"What's wrong?" Celeste asked, landing in a flourish on the bed.

"Um." Lulu looked embarrassed. "Celeste, it's not an emergency or anything like that, but I do want to ask you something."

"What?" Celeste asked eagerly. "I'll do whatever I can."

"Well, all of us in the Angel Club have been thinking about Derek and his bookstore," Lulu began. "He still doesn't have a sign on it, and the grand opening is tomorrow. Do you think you can help him?"

"I'll take care of it," Celeste promised. "You go to bed and don't worry about it."

"What will you do?" Lulu asked eagerly.

"Wait and see." Celeste smiled. "Remember: some surprises are better than others."

Lulu smiled back.

"Sweet dreams," Celeste said, offering Lulu a chocolate kiss.

With Celeste singing and the sweet taste of chocolate in her mouth, Lulu quickly fell asleep.

Her angel whispered good night in her ear and slipped a silver ring on Lulu's finger. It glittered with a diamond star, matching the one on her own angelic finger, except that in every shiny facet was an image of Celeste.

Celeste flew out the window and soared over to Derek's bookstore. It was very late, and nobody was on the street.

She waved her hand over the entrance to Derek's store.

Instantly, a sign lit up. Crystal letters as glittery as stars spelled out:

ANGEL CORNERS
CELESTIAL BOOKSTORE

Celeste smiled at her handiwork. "I've always wanted to see my name in lights."

Watching from the Crystal Classroom, all the angels-in-training applauded Celeste's work.

Amber gazed down, feeling happier than she had in ages.

Now there would be no more waiting! She was definitely the next angel-in-training who would visit Angel Corners.

Fran Manushkin is the author of more than thirty children's books. A native of Chicago, and formerly a teacher and children's book editor, she now lives in New York City with her cats, Niblet and Michael Jordan.